The Amber Ring

A.L. Walton

Acaleph Media

Gryphon line art by Seamartini Graphics

THE AMBER RING
First Edition (Trade Paperback)
ISBN-10: 0-615-78840-8
ISBN-13: 978-0-615-78840-1

FICTION / Fantasy

For the Bakers. Always helping me cook up a good story.

Keep looking for that crack in the rock.

-Part I-

The Girl and the Gryphon

So much trouble from such a little thing.

Maya turned the small golden band over in her palm, staring listlessly at the hardened orange resin in its setting. She thought she might hate it, if she knew how, but Maya Corona had never been very good with feelings. At least not the big ones.

Hueca, her grandmother called her. Hollow. Something missing on the inside. Even as a baby she had rarely laughed, rarely cried, and had broken the habits altogether by the time she took her first steps. Maya didn't really mind the moniker. She fancied herself a rational person, and sentimentality would only be an impediment to that conviction.

She was alone in the living room. Her grandmother was upstairs, and her parents were still at work. Now was as good a time as any.

She opened the grate over the fireplace and set a log within it, then retrieved the matchbook from the endtable by the couch. She withdrew a match, struck it, and tossed it into the pit.

The flames came quickly to life, roasting the air before her. She palmed Sofia's ring and tightened her hand around it, gazing at the flickering, volatile brightness. Then she loosened her grip and looked one more time at the soft golden gleam in her hand.

And she took the ring in her fingers. And held it above the fire. And took a deep breath.

The click and creak of the front door sounded behind her. She quickly pocketed the ring and turned to see her father step in, closing the door behind him and tossing his jacket onto the back of the couch. "Hey," he said simply.

"Hello, Papá," she replied.

"Mamá will be home soon. Want to help me make dinner?"

"O.K.," she agreed, then ducked her head and made for the kitchen, the ring pressing rudely against her through the side of her jeans.

"I would have cooked," Maya's mother said at the dinner table as her father served them all a hefty portion of chopped pork and rice.

"It's fine, *mi amor*." He sat down to eat with them. "It was a simple recipe." His mouth turned up a little. He had not smiled once since Sofia died, though his lips did often enough.

"It smells wonderful," her mother complimented. She did smile. She had been more energetic than ever in these last five months. She had taken her old job back as a grocery store manager, and did whatever she could to fill the time she was not working, picking up a new hobby every other week. "How was work?"

"Busy," her father responded. "We're still having problems rebuilding the contact database." He was a 'network administrator', whatever that meant. Something to do with computers. He looked over to his own mother, who was neglecting her meal for the small tablet computer in her hand. He had gotten it for her last Christmas for reading and playing word games. *"Mamá. No durante la cena, por favor."*

She looked up at him over her glasses. *"Sí, sí..."* She reluctantly set the tablet aside and began eating.

"And how about school?" Maya's mother asked her.

"Boring," Maya shrugged lightly. She used to like school, though she couldn't really remember why. She did well at it, all things considered, but little about it interested her anymore. Starting middle school without Sofia certainly didn't improve things. She used to help her twin with schoolwork, and that was something that made her feel useful. Maybe not excited, but useful. Sofia was always the outgoing, excitable one. Maya was more comfortable in the background.

"Just make sure to do your best," her mother smiled.

"Yes, Mamá."

Her grandmother had picked up the tablet again, tapping away intently at its screen. Her father noticed this, watching distantly for a moment, but went back to eating and said nothing.

Maya sat at the edge of her bed with her math homework in her lap, scrawling out the answers in monotonous succession. With every stroke of her pencil, she could feel another brain cell dying. She glanced out her window, toward the vast Oregonian woodland that comprised her back yard, then set her schoolwork aside and stood before the small oval mirror on her wall.

In a perverse sort of way, it was like being able to look at Sofia again. The near-black hair, meticulously straightened, framing her face in the front and falling to her shoulders in the back. The soft brown eyes. The silver chain necklace with its leaf token.

Of course, Sofia had preferred much livelier clothing. Maya never had much of a fashion sense; her wardrobe consisted of little other than jeans and plain-colored T-shirts. She never wore anything with logos or pictures if she could avoid it – they just seemed odd and tacky.

Maya didn't feel like she'd been a very good twin. Sofia and she had never developed a secret language, nor shared any kind of empathic bond. Their interests had always been different. Even now, after Sofia's death, Maya felt no lingering, immutable connection to her departed sister. No echo of her presence still within her. Where there should have been sadness at so profound a loss, Maya knew only emptiness.

Hollowness.

And there was Sofia's ring. She pulled it from her pocket and examined it once more. It had put more distance between Maya and her sister than anything else ever could have. Their grandmother had bestowed it upon them when they were only four years old, having inherited it herself as a child.

Does she even know what it is? Maya had never been able to bring herself to ask. Sofia had naturally been the one to learn to use it, and Maya did not begrudge her keeping it. It would only be jewelry in her hands.

If only Sofia had taken it with her when she went to the lake...

A quiet scrabbling sound outside the window caught Maya's attention. She pocketed the ring again and stepped over to look out. Seeing nothing noteworthy, she turned away.

Then a soft rapping pulled her back around.

She jumped, her mind swimming with a jumble of thoughts when she beheld the large avian head peering up from beneath the windowpane. When it popped back down, she slipped over and peeked through the glass.

On the deck outside stood a queer sort of creature – a lion with the wings and foreparts of a spotted eagle. An impressive black-dipped beak and eyes the same hue as the centerpiece of Sofia's ring adorned his noble aquiline head. Deep brown feathers striped occasionally with white trailed down his back, dipping to cover his outer thighs and ending in a fan above his lion's tail. His fur was a lush bronze, accented by a muted tan on his toes and underside, blending smoothly with the cream-colored feathers on his breast. All features Maya knew well.

She slid open the window as quietly as she could. "Camden?"

The gryphon stepped back on the deck, bowing his head a little. "Hello, Maya."

Maya furrowed her brow, then quickly put on her grey tennis shoes and climbed out the window, closing it behind her. "What are you doing here? I haven't seen you since..."

Camden looked away, and she didn't need to say anything more.

"I—I know." He looked ashamed. "I didn't think you'd want to see me. I didn't think it was my place to try and...I just thought..." He took an unsteady breath.

Maya sat down on the deck, leaning her back against the house, and nodded. In many ways, she understood, Sofia's death was probably harder on him than anyone. Sofia was everything to him. She had woven him out of nothing but love and imagination, and he had thereafter been her constant adventuring companion. He was the one who had helped her defeat the Cedar Witch and save the Fairwoods. He was for her what Maya couldn't be.

That was probably why she might have grown to resent him a little.

"When was the last time you saw her?" Maya asked over her knees.

"The...the week before." Camden sat too, stretching his wings a bit. "I felt it, when it happened. Like my heart was ripped out and crushed. By the time I could come for her, her body had already been found and taken away. I never got to..." He cast his gaze downward.

Maya said nothing for a while, simply looking him over. She had never really gotten the concept of a gryphon. Half-bird, half-mammal – how did that even work? His dark grey forelegs were effectively an eagle's hind legs, which seemed inherently strange. And the ears – why ears on an eagle head? They weren't even lion ears. More like...wolf or lynx ears. Large, pointy, and expressive. But, she supposed, if you were already intent on smushing two animals together, borrowing a part from one more wouldn't be out of the question.

Despite her qualms with the nature of his being, she did have to admit that there was a certain majestic artistry to the way it all somehow worked together, particularly as he had grown from the cub Sofia had crafted. And he was yet to fill out to full lion size. If nothing else, she did secretly find it pleasant to listen to the rich, gentle timbre his voice had gained.

"Why come now?" Maya finally asked.

Camden sighed, looking back toward the forest. "I know this is probably the last thing you want to hear, but...the Fairwoods are in trouble again."

"Trouble?" Maya frowned, following his gaze. "What kind of trouble?"

"The goblin kind. Over the last few weeks they've started raiding again."

"I thought the goblins turned peaceful once Sofia got them out from under the Cedar Witch's control."

"They did. But...I guess something must have changed."

"What are you going to do?"

"I was hoping..." He closed his eyes and exhaled, lowering his head and shaking it slowly. "Maya, I know this is a lot to ask, especially after everything that's happened, but we could really use your help."

"Me?" Maya raised an eyebrow. "There's nothing I can do. I'm not Sofia. I'm not the Heroine."

"You're her sister. You have the ring."

"I'm not a weaver. You know that."

"You could be," he said quietly, hopefully.

Maya stood up. "No, I couldn't. I'm sorry."

The gryphon regarded her another moment with wide, pleading eyes, then averted them and nodded, ears flattening. "I understand." He turned, and she watched him trod down the steps of the deck. He stopped at the bottom and looked back. "It was good to see you again, Maya."

Maya's mouth twitched, but she said nothing as he made his forlorn trek back to the trees. It was a shame the Fairwoods were in danger again after all the work Sofia did, but truly, nothing good could come of Maya stepping in and pretending to be something she was not. And getting involved in fairytale adventures was the last thing she wanted. She had to grow up and move on with her life, since that was something her sister would never have a chance to do.

As Maya half-attentively filled out the answers to her history test, she found her eyes drifting toward the clock above Ms. Patch's desk, subconsciously counting down the minutes, as she often did, until the tedium of the school day was over.

Her wandering eyes also noticed Braden Thomas, who sat at the desk to her right, surreptitiously sneaking a glance at her paper in regular intervals. She contemplated calling him out, or even writing down the wrong answers on purpose, but then decided to just let him cheat. If he could get through school without bothering to learn anything for himself, he would be one less person to pose her any real competition for an eventual job, which everyone was always saying was hard to get these days.

As she shifted to give him a better view of her exam, she felt something grind against her leg. It was Sofia's ring; she had left it in her pocket.

Her mind went unwillingly to the previous night. It had been strange to see Cam again. To think of him without Sofia. His charismatic pluck replaced with that crestfallen timidity. Maya wanted to leave the Fairwoods behind her, and had expected them not to think twice about returning the favor. Her involvement had been limited to the occasional tag-along with her sister, and she had never done anything of importance there. She had been clear on where she stood, though, hadn't she? Would they leave her alone, now?

"Two minutes," Ms. Patch droned.

At the edge of her vision, Maya saw Braden gripping his pencil tightly, throwing nervous glances her way. Quickly, to his obvious relief, she scribbled down the remaining answers to the test.

Sometime after dinner, Maya found herself standing before the lake behind her home. It was a quiet, wooded, ten-minute walk from the house. One her sister had made many times. One of the last things she'd ever done.

At the age of ten, Sofia Corona, Heroine of the Fairwoods, had saved the enchanted land from the twisted whims of an evil witch. Two years later, she had slipped, hit her head, and unceremoniously drowned in her own back yard.

Maya sat on the old oak stump a few yards from the shore. It had been her sister's favorite spot. The two of them had often sat there while Sofia would describe her adventures. Maya would listen politely, until Camden would come and take her attention away.

She fiddled with the silver leaf chain around her neck. Sofia had worn an identical one, both given to them by their late grandfather, but the lake had washed Sofia's away before her body was found. There was nothing magical about that necklace. Maya wished she could have had it instead of the ring.

She pulled the golden band from her pocket, passing it back and forth between her hands as she stared into the water's surface. Maybe it belonged at the bottom of the lake along with the chain.

But she didn't throw it in. Instead, for some reason, she slipped it on. Turning it slowly around her finger, she tried to reach out, in this all-important place, to feel her sister's presence. But nothing came. No ethereal voice, no spectral hand, no reassuring wind touched her mind.

There was, however, the sound of rustling movements behind her.

Maya stood and turned. She saw several figures stepping out from the trees, stalking toward her. They were between four and five feet tall. Holding spears and knives. Clad in rough scraps of leather. Skin smooth, green, and tattooed.

Goblins.

She had never seen one in person, but Sofia's descriptions had been clear enough.

"The ring," one of them whispered.

"It's her," another snarled.

They were hairless creatures. A small pair of slit nostrils in place of a nose. They had little fangs, large red eyes, and even larger, lanceolate ears. They were actually kind of cute, Maya thought strangely, as they advanced on her with unmistakable menace.

"Where is it?" the one in lead demanded, aiming his spear squarely at her.

Maya glanced over the goblin troupe, then behind herself, as if they were addressing someone else. "What?"

"*Where is it?*" the goblin repeated, thrusting his spear in warning and stalking closer.

Maya took a small step backward. She might have been afraid, were she not *hueca*. The bizarre, unexpectedness of the situation was too much for her to rationalize. Her mind drifted to the ring, and with an idle afterthought she tried to manifest a weapon as Sofia might have done.

Nothing happened, of course.

"Give it over if you value your skin!" another goblin warned.

She took another step back. "What are you talking about...?"

A couple goblins had apparently gotten around her, and grabbed her roughly by the arms. "You know what!" the lead goblin hissed, putting the spear's tip to Maya's throat.

"Do I?" Maya sighed tiredly. She found herself with diminishing motivation to fight against whatever it was that was happening. Maybe it was fitting that she would die here. In the same place her twin had spent her final moments. Her favorite spot. The thought didn't bother her all that much.

But a fearsome squall pierced the night air, and Maya looked up to see Camden dive into an impressive slide of a landing behind the goblin troupe.

"Crap, it's the gryphon!" one of them yelled. A few of them ran off in opposite directions, but the others turned away from Maya to face down the intruding beast.

"Kill him!" the leader screamed, charging.

None of them stayed back to guard Maya. That was pretty dumb. They probably could have held her hostage to keep Cam in check.

Camden crouched low as the goblin leader closed in, spear poised to strike. Pivoting to one side, the gryphon snatched the spear's shaft in his beak and wrenched it away, pulling the goblin still clinging to it to the ground and pinning him down with a talon.

The second goblin jumped in with a pair of knives. Cam thwapped him on the back with a wing, then raked him across the face with his free claws as he stumbled forward. The goblin fell to his knees, grabbing at his head and screaming as blood streamed between his fingers.

Cam roared and swept the pinned goblin away, then pounced on another. The unlucky green warrior crunched loudly under the gryphon's force, and stopped moving.

One more tried to sneak up from the side, thrusting at Camden's flank. The gryphon reared just in time, dodging the blow, then came down on the goblin's weapon, shattering it. He let out a screech an inch from his assailant's head, and the goblin turned and ran.

When the last able-bodied warrior thought it best to flee alongside his companion, Camden returned to the one clutching his face. The goblin trembled as the gryphon neared, squinting up at him through dripping red.

"Go," Cam snarled.

The goblin started, but jumped up and back, turning to run into the woods, falling several times along the way.

As soon as he was gone, Cam's fierce, feral façade dropped and he turned to Maya with enormous concern. "Are—are you O.K.? Did they hurt you? I got here as soon as I could – please tell me they didn't hurt you. I'm sorry, I didn't, I never—"

"I'm fine," Maya said, holding up her hands. Camden closed his eyes, relaxing visibly. She squinted. "How did you know to come here?"

Cam studied her a moment, his ears drooping, then he looked away. "I felt it. That you were in danger. I guess…I guess there's still some kind of connection there. Since Sofia's…"

"Oh," Maya murmured, and sat down in the grass. *Great*, she thought. *Here it comes*. Camden had saved her life, and now she owed him. She had seen first-hand what kind of trouble the Fairwoods were facing (not that it seemed to pose him much of a threat). Now he could ask her again to help him, and she would be obligated to do so. All because she had to make some stupid nostalgia trip down to this lake.

"I haven't been back here…" Cam murmured, regarding the lake with a sickly sort of stare. He looked down, then took a few tentative steps toward her, gingerly lifting a talon. "I, um…" Maya stared at the outstretched arm, and he lowered it abashedly. "Things might be dangerous around here for a while. You should probably stay close to home." He swallowed, and though he kept a respectful distance, she could tell by his longing gaze that he wanted to be closer. "I'll do another sweep around, but it should be safe for you to walk back." Then he turned to head into the woods. "If...if you ever need anything, I won't be far."

Her brow furrowed as she watched him go. Was that it? No guilt trip? Not even a mention of her potential to help? Maybe he realized she wouldn't be that useful after all.

Maya glanced toward the pair of goblin corpses, considering how fairytale fights could be just as ugly as any other. She wondered what would become of them – she could see them because of the ring, but most people would never know they were there. Would they just rot by the lake unnoticed, forever? What had they wanted, anyway? She had to remind herself that it wasn't her concern.

She stood slowly and began the walk back home, squeezing uncertainly at the ring around her finger.

Maya returned home from school the following afternoon, deposited her backpack in her room, then perused the kitchen for something small to snack on. She had settled on a granola bar when her grandmother called to her from the living room.

"*Ven aquí, niña,*" she beckoned without looking.

Maya made her way over to the small recliner her grandmother was wedged in. She was staring at her tablet through her thin rectangular spectacles, brow furrowed in focus under her short grey-streaked curls. "*¿Sí, Abuelita?*" Maya prompted.

Her grandmother pointed to her tablet screen. She was playing an electronic game of Scrabble, and was sixty-some points behind. "*Dame una palabra buena.*"

Maya studied her grandmother's tiles for a bit, then took a look over the playing board. Finally, she pointed to an open J. *"Equipaje."*

The old woman's eyes widened and she made a popping sound with her lips as she slid the tiles into place. *"Perfecto."* She snickered as her score shot thirty points ahead of her opponent's. *"Gracias, hueca mía."*

As Maya turned to head back upstairs, her grandmother caught her by the arm, staring at her hand.

"El anillo..." she said quietly.

Maya followed her gaze to Sofia's ring, then looked back to her face. Her grandmother squeezed her hand gently between her own, and offered a small smile, wistful and approving. Maya sighed and looked away, and when her grandmother let go, made quickly for the stairs.

"Looks...right on you," her grandmother observed in her wake.

Maya stopped briefly, turning halfway toward her, then headed back up to her room.

Plopping down onto her bed, she nibbled at the granola bar, unable to avoid her mind's track back to Camden and the Fairwoods. Why was she still wearing the ring? Why did she keep thinking about all of that when she wanted nothing to do with it?

Maybe it was just some uppity pull of fate twisting events around her to badger her into fulfilling its own self-interested whims. If there were a place where witches and goblins and gryphons could exist, it wouldn't be too much of a stretch to expect something like that could be at work, she figured.

But what if there really were something she could do? What if the only way to get past this preoccupation once and for all was to confront it and get it over with? If she could do this one thing, whatever it was, then perhaps she could truly and finally leave it all behind her. She could pay her dues and let it rest. Let Sofia and her memory rest.

Maya finished the granola bar, then crumpled the wrapper and tossed it toward her trash bin. It missed. She stared at it for several seconds, then slid off her bed and flopped onto the floor to plunk it in point-blank.

It was Friday. Monday was Labor Day. She supposed she could commit to giving it a three-day weekend. What she could do, she would do, and come Monday night, she would go home, and never have to deal with the Fairwoods or the ring again.

By the time her father got home, Maya had put on a new pair of grey jeans and a black shirt with a purple stripe around each sleeve (stripes were…O.K.). She had also stuffed her backpack with a few changes of clothes, her English homework, and some more granola bars. She imagined there would be food in the Fairwoods, but, just in case.

"Hi, Papá," she greeted as she headed down the stairs. "Allie asked if I could spend the weekend camping with her family." It was the excuse Sofia had typically used. Allie had been a long-time friend of the twins at school, and they would occasionally stay over with her family (though not nearly so often as their parents were led to believe). In truth, Maya had not spoken to Allie since the funeral.

Her father's mouth turned up a bit and he nodded. "Of course. That sounds wonderful." Maya knew he would just be relieved at the thought of her wanting to go out and do something. "Would you like me to drive you over?"

"No, thanks, Papá; I'll walk."

A look of mild anxiety crossed his features, but he inclined his head again. "Promise me you'll be careful, then."

"O.K." She gave him a quick, awkward hug, then went to open the front door. "I'll be back Monday night."

After following the sidewalk for a few minutes, she turned and veered back into the woods. She figured the lake would be the easiest place to go, despite what had happened the night before. The goblins probably weren't stupid enough to try the same thing twice, anyway.

Probably.

When she reached the shore, she set her backpack down on the old stump and twisted at Sofia's ring, glancing uncertainly around the vicinity. She was a little surprised to see that the goblin bodies from the previous night had been removed, after all. "Camden?" she asked the forest.

She wasn't really sure what she was doing.

"Cam?" she called, a little louder. Then she sat and waited, tenth-guessing her resolve.

Eventually, however, the gryphon appeared, loping through the trees and curiously entering the clearing. "Maya? Is everything all right?" He looked around. "What are you doing back here?"

"I'll do it," she mumbled.

"You'll...you'll what?" He tilted his head, ears perking, daring to hope.

"I'll...help you and stuff."

His bright orange eyes lit up, his feathers puffing slightly. "Really?"

"I guess."

"That's great!" He spun in a circle and bounded up to her like a puppy, but stopped short as she tilted back in surprise. A nervous chuckle escaped his beak as he recomposed himself. "What changed your mind?"

Maya shrugged. "I don't know. I just thought if I agreed to offer my help this one time, for Sofia's sake, I would never have to see or hear about any of this fairytale nonsense again. So, you have me until Monday."

"Oh..." Camden averted his eyes, excitement sinking to heroically masked dejection. "Well...we'd better get moving, then."

It was possibly not the nicest answer she could have given, particularly to one such element of said fairytale nonsense, but guilt was just one of the many emotions she had never been good at feeling.

"Do you have a coat?" Cam asked her.

"I'll be fine." It was still a reasonable enough temperature outside, and Maya had never really minded the cold otherwise. She picked up her bag and stepped up alongside him. "Where do we go, first?"

The gryphon watched her anxiously as she approached, then shifted his demeanor to dutiful. "I need to meet up with someone in the Mellow Meadow. We should also talk to its mayor; it was just hit hard by goblins." He hesitated a couple seconds before adding, "We could fly, if you'd like."

"Absolutely not."

Cam swallowed, looking away before forcing a smile. It was a little surprising, the amount of subtle expression she could read in the muscles behind his beak. "Just, um...follow me, then."

Maya inclined her head, and with one more glance back toward home, followed her sister's companion through the veil and into the Fairwoods.

-Part II-

The Requisite Quest

The mayor of the Mellow Meadow, as it turned out, was a bear.

Of course it was.

"Has the Heroine come back to us?" the bear, whose name was probably Benny or Barney, hoped when the two approached him.

"Mayor Burly," Cam greeted with a bow of his head. "This is Sofia's sister, Maya." He smiled a little, trying to keep upbeat. "She's agreed to help us."

"Her sister." The bear puckered his lips and nodded thoughtfully. "Well, I'm surely glad to meet any sister of the Heroine of the Fairwoods." He held out a large black paw.

Maya glanced to Camden, then took the bear's paw in both hands and shook it gently. "How does a bear become a mayor?" she couldn't help but ask.

Burly angled his head, looking upward. "Well..." He crossed his arms and scratched his chin. "I suppose it's because I'm the biggest." He nodded approvingly to himself. "And the bigger you are, the more little folk you can look after." This mayor had a rumbly voice and a contemplative manner, and was clearly pleased with his own importance.

"How many goblins came through this morning?" Cam asked, seemingly anxious to get things on track.

The bear made odd gestures with his paws while staring down at them. Counting, Maya realized after a moment. "At least five pawfuls." He slumped and sighed. "They were going where they weren't invited, and hurting the little animals. And stealing things, even after I asked them *very nicely* to leave." His brow pinched inward and he shook his head. "Then I roared at them, and I *don't* like roaring, because it scares the little animals. I even did it very loudly, but that only made them poke at me with their sticks." His lips puckered up again. "I tried to swipe at them and shoo them away, but then they put a net over me, and trapped me until they were done being menaces and left."

"Did you find out what they wanted or where they went afterward?" Maya inquired.

Burly lowered his head miserably. "No..." He pawed at the grass. "I'm not a very good mayor, am I?"

Cam put a talon reassuringly on the bear's shoulder. "You did the best you could. I'm sure those goblins would have done things even nastier if you hadn't been there."

"Thanks, Camden." The bear slipped his powerful arms around the gryphon's slim frame and squeezed – a little too hard by the strained look on Cam's face. "You're always so nice."

"Anytime," Camden rasped, ruffling a little as the bear let him out of his embrace.

"Should we find out if the other animals know anything?" Maya suggested. If she were going to involve herself in this problem, might as well approach it systematically.

"No need!" answered a vaguely familiar voice behind her. "I've already made the sweeps."

She turned to see the smirking visage of a satyr, chewing on a smoking pipe. He started a bit when he took in her face, but then removed his pipe and grinned widely.

"Maya! Been a while, been a while. Would have thought you were your sister if not for that serious expression." He snapped his fuzzy fingers. "Good to see you back in these parts."

Kallot, the name came back to her. He was something like a sheriff, as far as she remembered. He had helped Sofia on many occasions, and Maya had met him on a few of her reluctant visits. He was a rangy figure, wearing only a sash which held a couple daggers, a wood flute (but not a pan flute, disappointingly), and some sort of badge. His goat legs were a dark earthy tone, his upper body fully furred in lighter browns and tans. He sported a goat's ears and horns as well, and his face was comprised of simple but handsome spritelike features.

"Is it?" was all she could think to respond.

"Of course!" The satyr took her around the shoulder and turned so they both faced Camden. "Glad you could make it too, buddy."

Cam eyed the arm around Maya, then began walking, prompting Kallot and Maya to follow. "What have you learned?" he asked the satyr.

"The goblins are *angry*; that much you can bet! They've been raiding across the countryside in force." He took a puff on his pipe, but there didn't seem to be any smoke. "Not like they were under the Cedar Witch, though. Those were organized strikes; this is a crazed rampage."

Cam shook his head, eyes narrowing. "After everything Sofia did for them... What could be their reason?"

Kallot shrugged. "Still collecting the variables. It's strange, though, isn't it? More than two years of peaceful independence, and now this. With no warning. Maybe they've fallen in with a new tyrant, or maybe they think they have something to prove...but any way you stick it, it doesn't feel quite right." He took another puffless puff on the pipe. "Something tells me there's a cat at the end of this one."

"A what?" Maya queried.

The satyr's brow lifted. "You know, when things aren't exactly as you expect? Like if you come across a river all dammed up, and you follow the dam thinking you'll see a beaver, but instead you find a cat at the end."

"That doesn't sound like anything that's ever happened."

"Ah, don't be so sure," he smirked, shaking the pipe a couple times toward her for emphasis.

"Is there even anything in that?" Maya folded her arms.

"Nah," he admitted, bringing it up before his eyes and turning it over thoughtfully. "It's just a little something Sofia wove for me. Makes me look more official, though, don't you think?" He winked, and slipped it into his sash.

Maya pursed her lips. *Just three days*, she reminded herself.

"We can't afford to overthink it," Cam refocused the conversation. "Not while they relentlessly attack the innocent. We need to take action. The goblin kingdom has shown time and again that they can't respect the rest of the Fairwoods, so...maybe it's time to consider a permanent solution."

Kallot tilted his head. "You have something in mind?"

The gryphon was silent for several seconds, then said, "The Morning Stone."

The satyr took a long breath, raising an eyebrow. "You're thinking...send them the way of the ogres?"

Cam nodded, and Maya asked, "What happened to the ogres?"

"A few hundred years ago, their population bloomed and they needed to expand their territory," Kallot explained. "Unfortunately, their method of doing so involved plundering the land and resources of nearby civilizations. They were a formidable force, and it didn't take long for the other races to realize they couldn't hold them off forever. And so, when diplomacy failed, they used the Morning Stone to sever the ogres' connection to the Fairwoods altogether." He sighed. "So the story goes, anyway. It's a bit of an extreme to jump to, but...I suppose it wouldn't hurt to have the leverage."

Maya furrowed her brow. "If you have something that can do this, what do you need me for?"

"Well, we'd have to find it, first. And to get it we'd need..." He patted her ringed hand.

"Oh." A magical artifact fetch-quest. She should have seen it coming. "I can't weave," she reminded.

"Not yet," Camden corrected. "But it's not really about the weaving. You're still connected to the ring; it lets you enter the Fairwoods and see all of us. It should allow you to retrieve the Morning Stone."

"But you don't know where it is?"

"It's in the Gilded Garden," Kallot stated.

"I thought you said—"

"We don't know where the Gilded Garden is," Cam clarified.

"At least not right now," the satyr added. "It...moves around."

That didn't sound like anything Maya wanted to deal with. "Is there anyone who *does* know where it might be?"

Kallot scratched his chin. "Gnarlington Gnibblemeister."

"Gnarlington Gnibblemeister...?"

"The geographer gnome," Camden elaborated.

"Yeah," Kallot nodded. "Gnarlington Gnibblemeister the Geographer Gnome could gleam how to get to the Gilded Garden."

"O.K.," Maya said slowly. "So where is he, then?"

The satyr and gryphon shared an awkward look.

Maya narrowed her eyes. "You don't know, do you?"

"Not...so much," Kallot admitted, affecting an apologetic grin. "He moves around, too. You might ask the Disagreeable Donkey, though."

"The Dis...?" Maya closed her eyes and rubbed at their corners. All of this gratuitous alliteration was bound to give her a migraine.

An agonizing alliteration ache.

…

"You should also pay a visit to the Maple Witch," the satyr suggested. "She might be able to help you with the weaving."

Camden cringed. "Maybe."

The Maple Witch, as Maya recalled, had once worked in league with the Cedar Witch, at least until Sofia had redeemed her of her wicked ways and convinced her to switch sides. Maya had never met her herself.

"Well." Kallot crossed his arms over his scrawny chest and lifted a foot, tapping his cloven-hooved toes against the ground. "Sounds like you've got a plan. And I've got duties to attend." He double-tapped his badge. "I'll stop by your den in a couple days to check out your findings. Lovely seeing you, Ms. Corona." He grinned and bowed dramatically to Maya, then winked, swiveled around, and marched off.

"I guess we ought to track down that donkey, then," Camden put forth.

"I guess," Maya agreed, but she wasn't about to hold out hope that a creature so named would be of any help.

It was past sunset when they reached the grove of the Disagreeable Donkey. He was a bristly black creature, white on his muzzle and chest, and he was chewing lethargically on the tall grass around him.

"Good evening," Camden hailed as they came upon him.

The donkey looked up, swallowing. "I'm not sure that it is."

"Heh, well…maybe not with all the goblins running about."

"They haven't bothered me, yet," the donkey shrugged.

"They're bothering a lot of other folk, though. That's sort of why we're here. This is Maya," he gestured toward her with a wing.

The donkey regarded her dubiously. "She looks like the Heroine."

"She's her twin sister. They're identical."

"Not *that* identical. The Heroine was a cheery girl. And more confident looking. And she wore prettier things."

Maya looked down at her clothes. She thought they looked fine enough.

Camden scratched the back of his neck. "Yes, um...anyway, we just had a quick question for you. Do you know Gnarlington Gnibblemeister?"

"I'm *acquainted* with him."

"Do you know where he is?" Maya asked.

"He moves around frequently."

Maya put her hands on her hips. "So...is that a no?"

"I didn't say that."

"You do know, then?" Cam prodded.

"I didn't say that, either."

"Well, what *are* you trying to say?" Maya pushed.

"Who's trying? I believe I was quite successful in telling you that the gnome moves around a lot."

"We already knew that. What we need to know is where he is now."

"You may *want* to know, but I very much doubt you *need* to."

"Then we would *like* to know where he lives."

"I figured out that much."

"So, are you going to tell us...?"

"Why wouldn't I?"

After a pause, Cam pressed, "Where does he live, then?"

"In his house."

"Where is his house?" Maya urged.

"It's where he can be closest to his research."

Maya sighed. "It would be a shame if you could give us a straight answer," she ventured.

The donkey flicked an ear. "I don't see why. I would think that would make things easier for you."

"It seems like you're not going to give us one."

"Don't be silly. I was just about to tell you that I have no idea what Gnarlington's researching at the moment. He could be anywhere."

Maya shook her head tiredly. "Then we'll be going. You've been a big help."

"I don't think you mean that."

"No, I don't." She turned and trod away, Camden following. "That was a waste of time," she said to him after a few minutes.

"Yeah...sorry." He eyed the ground in disappointment.

"Should we see the Maple Witch, then, like Kallot said?"

Cam's feathers ruffled slightly. "Maybe in the morning. It's getting late; we'd better rest for the night."

They picked a small clearing to camp out in. Camden curled up under one tree while Maya sat with her back against another. She rummaged through her backpack and pulled out her English textbook, a sheet of college-ruled paper, and a pencil.

"What's that?" Cam asked, all friendliness, lifting his head and tilting it curiously.

"Homework," she said simply, keeping her eyes on it. Cam's beak wavered a little, but he seemed to see that she didn't want to talk, and laid his head back down.

Maya had never developed any respect for the notion of homework. What were her seven daily hours of school for? Her teachers would sooner belabor the same rudimentary concepts or chat about their social lives than use class time in anything resembling an efficient manner, and that somehow gave them a free pass to offload their job for her to do on her own time. And it was always just redundant, repetitive busywork.

Still, she had to do it, and this once it was almost a welcome distraction from all the fairytale absurdity going on around her. A small reminder of the normal life she was already anxious to get back to. At least it was something that would contribute toward her future, if only in the most vacuous of ways.

Her assignment for the weekend was to write an essay on Jack London's classic, "To Build a Fire." She briefly considered her surroundings and circumstance, and tried not to make any connections.

Maya awoke to a scratching, scrabbling sound and the sight of a dozen dark shapes scurrying away.

She blinked a couple times. They were shadowy rodent-like creatures, two feet long with glinting orange eyes. And they had her backpack.

"Hey..." she called, standing. She took a step toward them, but quickly stumbled over from vertigo and sleep-cramping. Camden's head snapped up and he blinked groggily, looking to her with concern. "My bag!" she pointed.

Cam glanced over. "Duskrats!" He hopped up and screeched. A few of the creatures scattered and sank under the ground, and Cam leapt toward the backpack. The remaining rats lashed out at him, scratching and biting and trying to keep their prize away. Cam swatted a few of them aside and managed to latch onto a strap with his beak.

"Don't let it go!" Maya grasped around for some stones, seizing a couple functional specimens and lofting them at the thieving creatures. One of them found a target, and its victim snarled in surprise before retreating beneath the earth.

Camden pulled fiercely back on the bookbag, but four of the duskrats had him locked in an unflinching tug-of-war. Two others harried his flanks, and another managed to land a solid swipe above his nares. He flinched, losing hold of the bag. He snorted in frustration, then growled and lunged back in, clutching for it with his talons, but they were already pulling it underground.

The duksrats snapped and clawed at the gryphon's face and forearms as he tried desperately to wrench the bag back up, until finally, despite Cam's struggles, it disappeared below the moss and dirt, the remainder of its abductors along with it.

Just like that, it was gone. Everything she had brought for the trip. She had just slept in the dirt, and would now have to wear the same thing for the entire weekend. She would have been furious if she were capable, but she didn't raise her voice when she said, "You let it go."

Cam was panting, staring despondently down at the spot where it had vanished. He turned slowly back toward her, not quite meeting her eyes. "I'm sorry, Maya...I—"

"Is it gone? For good?"

He swallowed and nodded. "No one gets anything back from duskrats."

"Did you know something like this could happen out here?"

He shifted, but said nothing.

"My clothes were in there, Camden. My food."

"I know, I—"

"The school assignment I just stayed up half the night to finish."

"I'm sorry," he repeated softly, clawing anxiously at the ground.

"You're sorry." She shrugged. "That's great. You're always sorry. What good does that do? What good has that ever done?" She folded her arms and shook her head. "If you can't even save a bag from being spirited away by a pack of rats right under your nose, it's no wonder you couldn't—"

She didn't finish that sentence. She didn't need to. Camden's ears drooped and his beak fell slightly open. He stared at her for a silent moment, his posture low and wounded, his eyes wide and pleading as blood trickled down from the worst of the rats' slashes. Then, he lowered his gaze, shut his eyes, and turned away. "Let's go see the Maple Witch." His voice was hushed, resigned.

Maya sighed. "Camden…"

"She lives a couple hours from here. An easy walk. Maybe she'll be able to get you something to eat."

The walk wasn't so easy. The terrain was smooth enough, but Maya could not say the same for the gryphon's demeanor. It was only a few minutes before he did his best to resume that ever-friendly composure, but she could still pick up a pronounced vulnerability underlying, and it made her uncomfortable. More so than she would have expected.

The awkward trek was eventually interrupted by the appearance of a winged white horse, descending through a sparsely-treed area to greet them.

"Welcome, travelers," the horse – or mare, to be precise – said.

"A pegasus," Maya murmured, somewhat impressed. Camden winced.

The mare slumped. "I am most certainly not *a Pegasus*."

"Oh…what are you, then?"

She raised her head. "A *volequus*, thank you very much."

Maya looked her over. "What's the difference?"

The not-a-pegasus whickered shortly. "Pegasus was simply a very famous volequus. But we are not like—like Kleenexes; you can't just refer to our whole species by the name of its most prominent member."

Maya thought it a little strange to hear a flying horse talk about Kleenexes, but she decided it better not to ask. She inclined her head. "I see. I'm sorry if I offended you."

The volequus sighed and shook her head. "I suppose it's all right. Common mistake and all." Then she examined Maya more closely. "You know something? You look familiar…" Her eyes settled on the ring and widened, and she took a step back. "The Heroine?"

Maya pursed her lips. "Her sister. Maya."

"Oh. Well, honored to meet you, Maya. I'm Nissa, personal companion to the Maple Witch." She bowed her head and fanned her wings, then addressed the gryphon. "Might you be the legendary Camden's brother, then?"

"Just Camden," Cam smiled faintly.

Nissa regarded him approvingly and folded in her wings. "Well, normally there are questions and procedures one must go through before they can see Her Mapleness, but I suppose we can skip all that for such esteemed guests. This way, if you please!" She turned and marched on, leaving Maya and Camden to follow.

The witch's cottage was tucked neatly away in a grove replete with her eponymous tree. Their leaves seemed to glow in the overcast sky, diffusing a soft red luminance throughout the area. It was strongly suggestive of autumn and Halloween, which Maya supposed was appropriate.

As they neared the door, the volequus cleared her throat and called, "Visitors, Madame!" A minute passed with no response. The mare shifted, then tried again, "Madame?"

This time, the door swung open, and the Maple Witch stepped out. "What is—?" Her bright green eyes widened when they took in the other two. She was an unexpectedly beautiful woman, with her long red hair, smooth skin, and slim black dress. She smiled pleasantly and held her arms out in welcome. "Cammy!" She crouched to embrace Camden. He tensed, but remained still as she stroked his back affectionately. "I just knew you'd come back to see me." She took his head in her hands and moved back a little. "How is my gorgeous little gryphon? You've gotten bigger, haven't you?"

"A little," he shrugged awkwardly.

The witch ruffled his head-feathers, then stood and faced Maya. "And you must be the Heroine's sister."

"Maya," she nodded.

"It's very nice to meet you, Maya. We're all terribly sorry about Sofia." She clasped her hands together and shook her head, her expression sobering for a brief moment. "Well, then, I am the Maple Witch, and this is my home – a home you are both more than welcome at. I see you've already met my pegasus."

Nissa slumped.

"She was very helpful," Cam said politely. "We were hoping you might be, as well."

The Maple Witch crossed her arms and smiled. "I couldn't bear to be anything less to the Heroine's sister and my pretty little Cammy." She brushed back her hair and Maya caught a glimpse of a pointed ear. The witches were greater elves, she remembered Sofia saying. "Please do come in."

The maple-leaf motif was ubiquitous within the witch's cottage. Everything Maya could see was imprinted with or shaped in its likeness. Even where – perhaps *especially* where – it would be least practical, such as the table in the main room's center.

When all but Nissa were inside, the witch closed the door and gestured for Maya to take a seat on a leaf-backed padded bench to one side of the table. "You must be hungry, coming all the way up here. Can I get you something to eat?"

Maya felt her stomach approve of that notion. "That would be nice. Thank you."

The witch pulled a wand from somewhere and waved it over the table. A shower of red and white sparks splashed before Maya, fizzling down and dissolving into a mist which in turn formed a generously portioned meal within its accompanying leaf-molded dishware. Maple sausage with maple syrup on maple bread. Maple tea to drink, and maple bars for dessert. It smelled too good for Maya to begrudge the excessive theme.

As Maya ate, the witch knelt down and played with Camden's ear. "And what about you, Cammy? Don't lie, now; you always were a big eater!" She rubbed his belly. Maya was beginning to see why Camden was reluctant to come here. The witch's doting on him even bugged her a little, though she couldn't quite say why – it wasn't some sort of possessive instinct, was it? She hastily dismissed that reasoning.

Cam shifted. "I guess so."

The witch patted him on the neck and conjured a large platter of sausage links before him, then took a seat at the leaf-table across from Maya. "I expect that this is about the goblins?"

Maya nodded. "Do you know anything about what they're doing?"

"Invading, pillaging. Who knows why? Maybe they've grown bold at your sister's death, and think no one will stop them this time."

"But Sofia helped them."

"She did. Freed them from my cousin's control. But... goblins will be goblins. They're opportunists." She shrugged a little. "I wouldn't spend too much time looking for a cat at the end."

"That's not a thing..." Maya grumbled to herself.

Camden looked up from his meal. "We're going to find the Morning Stone, and use it to break their connection to the Fairwoods."

"Are you, now?" The witch raised an eyebrow. "I suppose they have it coming, if they can't be trusted to play nice with others." She eyed Sofia's ring. "I bet they weren't counting on another weaver coming so soon."

Maya managed to avoid rolling her eyes. "I'm not a weaver."

"But I think she can be," Cam insisted. "And maybe you could teach her something about how."

"Can you weave?" Maya asked the witch.

"Afraid not. A witch deals in witchcraft," she admitted, regarding her wand as she twirled it. "That doesn't mean I don't know a thing or two about how weaving works, mind you. A witch's and weaver's power both come from nature. That's why my cousin so resented your sister. Truth be told, she wanted Sofia's power for herself."

"Why? It doesn't seem like a witch is lacking in power."

"Weavers draw their power from where it is most concentrated – the preserved essence exuded directly from its ancient arboreal sources." The Maple Witch stood and took a few steps. "It lets them do things that we cannot."

Maya looked at the resin on her finger. "Like what?"

"Create life." The witch lowered herself next to Camden again, putting an arm around him and running her hand down his side. "From their will alone. They can bring forth into this world a creature as beautiful and perfect as they desire, with a beating heart, a thinking mind, and a feeling soul." She placed her other hand on the gryphon's chest, gazing fondly over him, marveling at his very existence. "Sofia used this power well." Cam looked away. She let him go, standing and turning back to Maya. "There are few who could refrain from abusing it. Perhaps that is why she was a weaver, and my cousin was a witch."

Maya regarded Camden a moment, turning the ring around her finger. She reminded herself again, with a hint of both bitterness and sympathy, that she would never understand her sister's loss the way he did.

The witch sat back down at the table, her face growing contemplative. "There was one who mastered both disciplines, a very long time ago. The Oak Witch. It's said she wove the whole of the Fairwoods with the very thing you're looking for."

"The Morning Stone?"

The witch bowed her head. "Magnificent power, the Oak Witch had, but even she could overreach. She became enraptured with creation. But also with control. You see, the Morning Stone remained a part of everything she created, and when you possess a part of someone, you hold influence over them. All in the Fairwoods were bound to her will, and she did not shy from exerting it. The strain required to maintain such control was enormous, however, and she refused to relinquish it. Some say it drove her mad, others that it drained her utterly, either way resulting in her own demise." The Maple Witch spread her hands. "Now, I won't say that we're not all better off with the bond broken and our ancestors' consequent freedom to claim their own destiny, but you see what I'm getting at – it takes a certain subtlety, an earnest compassion, to use such an ability wisely."

Maya wasn't quite sure how to respond to all of that, so she took a sip of her tea.

"Now, you wish to learn the secrets of weaving for yourself."

"If you think it will help," Maya consented with reluctance. "Though I don't think I'll be any good at it."

"Nonsense. Sofia was a natural. And while you may be a little older than most to just be starting out, weaving really is quite simple for those who have the connection. It merely requires the harnessing of emotion and the focusing of imagination."

Maya sighed. She might as well have just said it required three eyes and four hands.

"Picture the flower, sprouting out from the pot," the Maple Witch said, a slight tension in her voice, several unsuccessful hours into her lesson.

Maya held her ringed hand out in front of her, staring intently at the soil-filled pottery on the table.

"Try to feel the natural energies flowing into the earth, using you as a conduit, the ring as a catalyst," the witch continued. "Think of something that makes you happy. Something that excites you. Something warm and pleasant and beautiful."

This was stupid. Sofia might have had an endless supply of emotional context to draw upon, but Maya was *hueca*. She simply wasn't cut out for this sort of thing. The witch had explained the basics well enough, but an intellectual understanding of a skill did not equate to proficiency in it – she knew all the rules of basketball, but couldn't make a shot if her life depended on it. After another moment lacking in spontaneous plant growth, she put her hand down. "I can't." She leaned back and folded her arms. "Sorry."

The witch frowned, putting her hands on either side of the pot. "You *can*. You're just not bel—"

"I hope you're not going to say 'believing in yourself'." Hokey banalities were certainly not going to get her anywhere.

The witch looked away. "I just mean, if you had a p—"

"Positive attitude?"

The witch's lips puckered.

"Maybe things are different here in fairytale-land, but in the rest of the world, *wanting something really badly* and *trying really hard* aren't enough to get it." She stood. "I'm sorry we wasted your time, but it just doesn't look like this is my thing."

Sighing, the witch stood as well, but then smiled. "It's never a waste of time to get to see Cammy."

The gryphon, who had been waiting patiently in the corner, rose and stepped up beside Maya. "I suppose we should get going, then. We still need to find Gnarlington."

"Gnarlington Gnibblemeister?" the witch asked.

"Gnarlington Gnibblemeister the Geographer Gnome," Cam confirmed. "He can help us get to the Gilded Garden."

"You don't happen to know where he currently lives, do you?" Maya ventured.

"No, but...I think I know just who might." The Maple Witch held up a finger. "I saw him at the Summer's End

Festival a couple weeks ago. He had on the loveliest new boots – said he had them delivered."

"By whom?"

"The Fairy Cobblers, of course!"

Of course. "And where are they?"

"I know the way," Cam said. "Too far for tonight, but we can rest at my den." He shifted. "No rats, that way."

Not that there was anything left to take, but Maya accepted the gesture with a nod. "It was nice to meet you," she said to the Maple Witch. "Thank you for the meal and the information."

"Anytime." She clasped Maya's ringed hand between hers for a moment. "Take care of Cammy." She knelt before the gryphon and cupped his face, stroking his cheeks with her thumbs. "He's a one-of-a-kind."

Maya found herself putting a hand on Camden's neck and guiding him toward the door. His eyes flashed toward her, as surprised at the voluntary touch as she was.

"Good luck," the witch offered as they made their exit. "And don't give up on the weaving. Practice what I've told you, and eventually you'll get it!"

Maya very much doubted that.

"Sorry if that was uncomfortable for you," Maya told Camden as they trekked to his den under the darkening sky, and was pretty sure she meant it.

"It's all right," he smiled, and almost added an affectionate nudge, but apparently thought better of it as he turned it into an awkward neck stretch. "We got some food and learned something useful."

Maya turned the ring around her finger. "It's too bad I'm not more useful."

Cam's expression turned concerned. "Don't blame yourself for that."

"I don't. Everyone just needs to take a step back and remember that I'm not the Heroine. I agreed to do what *I* could to help, but I can't do what my sister could do." She lifted her shoulders. "If anyone is expecting another Sofia, they're going to be disappointed."

"Whatever you can or can't do...I'm just glad you're here, Maya," Cam said softly, with such excruciating sincerity in his gentle voice that it shut off any avenue of retort.

Then Camden stopped suddenly, ears perking, eyes widening, head lifting and panning. He sniffed the air, then let out a growling screech, flaring his wings and positioning himself defensively in front of Maya. "Get down!"

Maya crouched, ears ringing from Cam's roar, and saw goblins emerge from the brush.

And giant weasels.

Goblins riding giant weasels.

Cam reared, and a rider collided with him. Maya stumbled away, crawling backward as the gryphon and weasel tumbled, tossing the goblin from his seat. Maya slipped between two thick birch trunks, uncertain if she could do anything to help, or if it would be better simply to stay out of the way.

Camden managed to pin the weasel as it twisted and scratched at him, but there were two others still with riders, and they were charging in.

Releasing his captive, he leapt at one of the others, earning a nasty gash to his thigh as the prone weasel snapped out in retaliation.

"Give it back," a voice hissed behind Maya.

She whirled around and was promptly seized by a goblin on foot. He shoved her back against one of the trees.

"What...?" She looked him over in mild incredulity.

"Give it back!" the goblin repeated through his teeth, his hot and prickly breath invading her nostrils.

This again. "Give what back?" She was more curious than anything.

"You know what!" He shook her, his red eyes trembling with a desperate sort of anger.

A gurgling screech diverted both of their attention. Camden had just torn out the throat of one of the giant weasels.

Maya looked back as the goblin gawked for another moment. He was holding her by the shirt with both hands, and had a dagger hanging from his belt. Good grief, these things were stupid.

She reached down and plucked out the dagger, then held the tip against the goblin's flat green abdomen. His eyes were drawn to the sensation and he sucked in a short breath.

She could stick it into him, she realized in that instant. Pierce through skin and muscle, maybe an organ or two. She could kill him, just like that. She could end another's life, with no way to take it back, and not even get in trouble for it. It was sort of a horrible thought, but was it not what she was supposed to do in a situation like this?

Maybe she lacked any good sense of self-preservation, or maybe it was just the innate surrealism of the Fairwoods, but she couldn't bring herself to feel threatened by the goblin. Even as he and his companions assaulted her and hers unprovoked, the thought of killing him just seemed so... extreme.

The goblin released her and stepped back, hand instinctively reaching for his dagger and grasping open air. The fury in his countenance melted away into fear.

Maya glanced down at the weapon she still pointed toward him. The handle was bone, the blade iron and shaped like half a teardrop. She twisted up her mouth. "You should probably run away," she told the goblin uncertainly.

He nodded a little, then did so.

Another cry directed her focus back to Camden – this one his own. Maya watched a goblin pull a spear from his flank, and then get his chest shredded open by the gryphon's talons.

Only the other two giant weasels remained, and they continued to harry Camden with vehement persistence. He was still managing to hold them off, but he wasn't looking so well.

Maya eyed the dagger again, thinking that she ought to do something. The weasels were not so tall as Cam, but they were longer, and lacked not a bit of ferocity. Definitely more dangerous than their goblin masters.

She hurried up behind one of them as it snaked back and forth, and held out the blade. "Stop it," she said firmly and loudly, as if chiding a misbehaving pet.

The weasel whirled around and lashed out its claws, striking the dagger and knocking it away.

"Oh," she muttered, disappointed, and began back-pedaling as it advanced on her instead.

Camden gasped and turned his attention fully toward that one, lunging out and latching his talons into the rear of its long flanks and snapping his beak into its rump. It shrieked and twisted away, bolting off into the woods, but the other took advantage of the distraction and tackled the gryphon's back, clamping its jaws around his neck.

Cam dropped and wriggled wildly, fighting to free himself, throwing his weight back onto his assailant and clawing up at its face. The weasel held on tight, tearing him up with all of its claws, forcing him down until a talon caught its nose and ripped.

The weasel snorted and let go, jerking back its head. Cam flipped around and cuffed its cheek, driving a knee into its belly and forcing it onto its back. The weasel clutched at Camden's shoulders with its forepaws, ducking its head, but the gryphon got his beak around its scruff. The two rolled twice in this position, Cam wrestling for purchase. Finally, on the third roll, he pinned a leg with a foot, a shoulder with a talon, and with one last great twist, he snapped the creature's neck.

Maya watched the brutal scuffle numbly, her mind still resisting the severity of it all, still refusing to acknowledge just how perilous a place the Fairwoods could be. Camden rose slowly, shakily from his kill. He was a mess. Wings drooped, limbs unsteady, gulping for air. Sleek red blood matted his fur and feathers, rolling freely down from countless wounds and pooling in the grass beneath him.

He swallowed and brought that familiar anxious gaze up to Maya. "Are you O.K.?" he croaked. She stepped cautiously toward him, only managing to bob her head.

She could smell his blood.

She had always thought that was something only animals could do; she had never realized how powerful the odor was in concentration. It was warm and musky, like the scent of his fur, but amplified, purer. It smelled at once of life and death.

Maya didn't know what to think, seeing him like this, seeing what he was willing to put himself through for her safety. What had she ever done, what could she ever do, to justify such unflinching devotion? "Can you...can you make it back to your den?" she forced herself to ask. She reached out, timidly, and placed her hand on the side of his neck, careful not to prod at any gashes.

The touch seemed to go some small way toward revitalizing him. "I think so," he panted, trying to compose himself, wincing as he rolled his shoulders. "It's not...it's not too far. I'll just have to...to move a little slower." He took a few tentative steps. Maya could see the jaw muscles behind his beak twitch as he swallowed the pain, but he carried himself without further complaint.

A glint on the grass caught Maya's eye as she moved watchfully alongside him, and she stooped down to pick up the trophy she had pilfered from the goblin. Better to have it than not, she decided, even if it were unlikely that she could bring herself to use it.

• • •

They made it to the den a little under an hour later. Cam's den – that seemed like something someone here would try to make a joke out of. She was glad there was no one else around to do so.

As they stepped through the entrance, Cam reached up and tapped something sternly with a talon. It began to glow, illuminating the area about as well as an incandescent bulb. Some kind of luminescent rock hanging from a string. Why not?

The den was the size of a large bedroom, a coil of pads and rags in the middle where the gryphon slept, and a myriad of trinkets and knick-knacks scattered around the edges on various tables and rock-shelves, all likely collected on his adventures with Sofia. An assortment of jewelry and clothing hung on a coatrack in the corner, capped with a fur-rimmed top hat candy-striped in lime and lavender and ornamented with a slapdash array of needlelike protrusions. Fairytale tackiness at its finest.

Camden sat, exhausted, and stretched gingerly, assessing his injuries. Then he stepped up to the water trough along one wall and plunked his head down, drinking deeply. Certain this time that she wanted to do something useful, Maya picked up one of the bed rags and dunked it in the water beside him.

"Let me help," she said, then began, as tenderly as possible, to mop the blood from his ravaged form. He murmured consent into the trough, and did his best to stay still while she worked.

She cleaned for a while in silence, and caught herself admiring how resilient a creature her sister had created. His sturdy bones, taut sinews, and lean, firm muscle tone. How indomitable he had to be to hold himself so well after such punishment. The least she could do, she supposed, was to see that the nobility within him was properly reflected on the outside.

Most of the cuts and scrapes had clotted over, but she saw that he was still bleeding from the worst of them when she blotted at them with the soaked rag. "Do you have any balm or gauze?" she asked. She had to imagine Sofia would have prepared for the dangers they often faced. But, then, maybe she just wove everything all better.

"Yeah." Camden looked toward the back of the den. "I'll get it."

"No, that's—"

But he was already making his way to the desk against the rear wall. He rummaged through the desk's large top drawer, then returned with a roll of bandage tape and a jar of ointment.

She took them from him and dressed the wounds as best she could. She was no expert, but she thought she did a pretty good job of wrapping what she needed to and putting pressure in the right places. The bleeding had stopped and the nastiest of the slashes were covered, anyway.

When she was done, Cam nuzzled her face, and whispered, "Thank you."

She looked away, but as he lay wearily down on his bed, she sat beside him to give him a once-more-over with the rag. "You're going to be O.K., right?"

He gave a slight nod, and smiled weakly. "Comes with the job."

Maya sighed, and stroked the gryphon's head. He closed his eyes and leaned into it, so content for that moment despite what he had been through to earn it. Feeling the pull of her own drowsiness, she leaned against him, appreciating the comfort of his softness and warmth. "You're not so bad, Cam," she mumbled into his feathers.

He slipped a svelte grey foreleg around her and pulled her in closer, letting a wing droop down over her like a blanket. She could feel the rise and fall of his chest and the steady drum of his heart – that perfect, loyal, selfless heart Sofia had crafted with her will and love.

It felt so...peaceful. She reached a hand up and ran it down Cam's neck. He really was a lovely creature, she admitted to herself, not even grudgingly. Why had she tried so hard not to see it? The gentle palette of browns and whites, the youthful gloss of his fur and feathers, handsome even in this worn-down state. The unspoken strength in his regal features. A predator and a protector, as fierce as he was caring. This ideal companion, this true friend, who would never judge her, always watch out for her, and want for nothing but her affection. Maya had envied him his superior connection with her sister, but there was perhaps another part of her that had always been jealous of Sofia for having him.

Think of something warm and pleasant and beautiful.

Maya held her hand out toward the trough, focusing on the surface of the water, and almost, *almost*, thought she saw it move.

• • •

Waking in a pleasurable sort of haze, Maya felt something wet against the side of her face. She shifted groggily, remembering where she was, and glanced up to see tears spilling silently down from the corners of Camden's closed eyes.

"Cam?" She reached out and palmed a cheek. He tensed up and his tail twitched, but he didn't open his eyes. "Cam?" she asked a little louder, cupping his face. He started, pulling away from her and standing, breathing sharply. Maya struggled to catch her balance from the sudden movement, then sat up. "Cam, what's wrong?"

He seemed to stare out into nothing, taking another deep breath, then he blinked harshly and shook his head. "I was just—I was dreaming of…"

"Sofia," Maya finished, when he couldn't.

He looked away. "It shouldn't have ended like that. I should have—"

"Cam…you can't blame yourself for what happened."

"How can I not? She needed me—"

"*Cam*. It's not your fault." It was strange to hear herself say that. She had not shied away from holding him responsible for failing at his duty.

"You don't understand." He shook his head again. "I…I was supposed to protect her, but…" His voice was quiet, distant. He dug his talons into the ground. "You should go. Maya, you should go home. I shouldn't have brought you here."

A day ago, she might have welcomed that sentiment. But now…

Maya stood and paced up to him, stepping around to look him in the eyes. "Listen. Sometimes...people are careless. They make just the wrong mistake at just the wrong time, and there's nothing anyone else can do about it. You can wish you were there; you can wish luck were kinder. You can think of a thousand little ways it might have gone differently, if only. *If only*. But eventually...you have to accept that it didn't." There was a small but noticeable relaxation in the tension throughout her shoulders. She may have wished to exonerate more than just Camden.

The gryphon's beak fell open, but then snapped shut along with his eyes. He sighed and lowered his head. "I wish I could tell her I'm sorry."

"We can both do that by saving this ridiculous place that she loved so much." Maya gently took his arm between her hands and squeezed it. "So come on. We apparently have some cobblers to see."

"Ho! Come in, come *in*!" exclaimed a boisterous little man in a tan shirt and maroon overalls, moments after Maya knocked on the door of his towering boot-shaped house. "Honey-bear, we have customers!" he called over his shoulder.

"What's that, sweetie-muffin?" a woman's voice came in return.

"Customers, cherry-doll, *customers*!"

The woman came quickly into view, rushing up to meet Maya and Camden as they stepped through the doorway. She wore olive overalls and a white blouse, and was clapping her hands together with excitement. "Not just *any* customers, lovey-cakes, but the Heroine of the Fairwoods herself!"

"Actually," Cam winced, holding up a talon. "This is her sister, Maya. Sofia's..."

"She's dead," Maya said bluntly.

The couple blinked, sharing a surprised look.

"We're very sorry to hear that," murmured the man, taking off his cap – which matched his overalls – and holding it against his chest.

"She was just the loveliest girl," the woman added, shaking her head at the floor.

After an awkward moment of silence, the man put back on his cap. "Well, we're glad to meet you in any case, Miss Maya." He pointed a thumb to himself. "I'm Pilder, the husband."

The woman copied the gesture. "I'm Hilma, the wife."

Together, they finished, "And we're the Fairy Cobblers!"

Maya stared for a moment. They were about goblin-height, these shoemaking spouses, and had pointed ears. They looked like they were perpetually on the edge of middle age. Lesser elves.

"Nice...to meet you," she managed, taking her first good look around the cobblers' combined home-and-workshop. Shoes were piled at every wall from floor to ceiling. Boots, sandals, clogs, loafers, heels, and slippers in all shapes and sizes covered every spare surface, spilling from shelves and closets and even the chimney.

What was it with fairy-types and shoes, anyway?

"See anything you like?" Hilma asked, noticing her eyes wander.

Maya found it hard not to gawk at the dizzying array of footwear. There must have been over a thousand pairs just within her sight. "There certainly are a lot of...shoes."

"Of course!" Pilder grinned, swinging a fist across his chest. "We're cobblers!"

"Are you stocking these all up for a large order?"

"Well...not exactly." The shoemaker shrugged abashedly, scuffing the floor with his boot. "It's only just...not a lot of Fairwoods citizens actually *wear* shoes, so...they sort of kind of pile up a little bit."

Maya raised an eyebrow. "If the shoes you have aren't getting taken, why keep making more?"

"Because we're cobblers!" Hilma cheered.

Maya exhaled lengthily.

"So!" Pilder clasped his hands together and rubbed them briskly. "Shall we get you fitted up?"

"Good thinking, sugar-loaf!" his wife chimed. "I'll get the big boy." She was already behind Camden, grabbing at his hind paws with measuring tape in hand. He looked back, startled, then tried to pull away gently, turning, but the elf woman spryly and persistently kept up.

"That's all right," Maya told the couple, holding up her hands. "We didn't come here to get shoes."

Pilder froze, his expression drooping. Then he laughed – a nasal, rickety sound – and tapped his foot. "Didn't come to get shoes, she says! Did you hear that, candy-bean? We've got a jokester on our hands! Ha! Ho! Didn't come to the cobblers for shoes! That'd be a real cat-at-the-end, wouldn't it?" He chuckled again and winked at Maya, then turned and knelt to start digging through piles of his product.

Maya twitched. "I'm...no, I really—we only came here to ask you a question. Just a question."

The cobblers both stopped what they were doing and shared a disappointed look. "No shoes?" Pilder asked, voice nearly despondent.

"No shoes," Maya confirmed.

Pilder rose and sighed dramatically, hunching his shoulders and slipping his hands into the pockets of his overalls. His eyes bored holes in the ground for several seconds, and then he took a sharp breath and looked back up to Maya, jolly composure suddenly regained. "All right, then! No biggie! What can we answer for you, Miss Maya?"

Maya cast a dubious glance back toward Hilma, who seemed to have undergone the same transformation, then asked, "Do you know Gnarble—Gnilling—er, Gnibling—"

"Gnarlington Gnibblemeister?" Camden saved her.

"The gnome geographer?" Hilma intoned.

"The geographer gnome, butter-button!" Pilder corrected.

Hilma put a hand to her chin. "I don't know, cookie-lumps, I swear it was *gnome geographer*..."

"Geographer gnome, coffee-bird! He's a gnome who is a geographer."

"But isn't he also a geographer who is a gnome?"

"He was a gnome before a geographer, I think you must agree!"

"So shouldn't gnome come first?"

"No, jelly-dove, *geographer* is the descriptor, the distinguisher, the—"

"Do you *know* him?" Maya interrupted.

"Oh!" Hilma touched her chest, smiling apologetically. "Yes, of course! We sold him the most dashingly dapper pair of boots just a few weeks back."

"And you delivered them to his house?"

Hilma clapped her hands. "We sure did!"

Finally, they were getting somewhere. "Can you tell us where he lives, then? We need to go see him."

The elf put on a pouty face and looked to her husband.

"Well, you see..." Pilder scrunched up his features, making fists and tapping his knuckles together. "The thing is...that's confidential customer information! We can't just go telling anyone that, even if you are the Heroine's sister..."

Maya sighed. "But you're the only ones we've found who seem to know his current whereabouts. It would be a very big help to us. I'm sure he wouldn't mind." He probably actually would, Maya had to imagine, but it seemed like the thing to say.

"It's about the goblins," Cam added. "He can tell us what we need to know to stop them."

"Goblins," Pilder grumped, nose reddening.

"Those dirty little devils stole half our leather supply," his wife mourned.

"And their blasted weasels killed our guard-pig, Spoinky." Pilder shook his head, raised an eyebrow to Hilma, who nodded, then turned a grin on Maya. "I'll tell you what, Miss Maya – maybe we can make a little fairy bargain. If you can answer us a riddle, then we'll tell you where ol' Gnarly hangs his hat."

"A riddle?" Maya echoed. That sounded like a hassle.

Pilder bobbed his head, then cleared his throat into his fist. "I'm not always right, but I'm never wrong. I have a tongue and a throat, but no mouth to speak of. I move better when tied up. What am I?"

Maya groaned, eyeing Camden with the expectation of shared incredulity, but saw him deep in concentration, mouthing the riddle to himself. "A shoe," she answered, pinching the corners of her eyes.

The cobbler blinked. "O.K. O.K., that may have been an easy one. You try, caramel-puff."

"Sure thing, vanilla-boo, I've got just the one!" Hilma pumped a fist, then gave Maya a devious smile. "You tread on my sole, yet—"

Maya cut her off, "A shoe. Are you a *shoe*?"

Hilma stood in silence, her mouth still hanging open, then folded her arms and nodded gravely. "Very clever, this one. I think she's got us beat, cricket-pie."

Even Pilder seemed to double-take at that one. "Yes, yes," he conceded. "Very well. We'll give you the gnome's current address. But on one condition – you must pick out a new pair of shoes to take with you! No charge, of course." He winked at his wife. "Do we have a deal?"

"You'll tell us what we need to know if I let you give me free shoes?" Maya slipped her hands into her pockets and shrugged. "Yeah, that sounds fine."

They reached the gnome's cabin a little after midday, as a chill began to set in. There was refreshingly nothing remarkable about the residence. Maya looked down at the black suede half-boots that had carried her there – much nicer for all this hiking than her tennis shoes had been. The cobblers knew their stuff, she had to admit.

"Do you think he'll really know where this garden is?" she asked Camden. "Or is this going to be another goose-chase?"

"Eagle-chase," the gryphon corrected, tapping his beak with a talon.

Maya turned her head toward him and stared.

He grinned sheepishly. "Kallot said the gnome would know; we just have to hope for the best. But either way," he nudged her, "we'll keep trying 'til we find it."

Maya knocked on the cabin's door and waited. An older gentleman answered, white-haired and bald-pated, with a bulbous nose and small round spectacles. He was of a size with a lesser elf, which made him a greater gnome. Maya was a little surprised at how much of this she remembered.

"I must be seeing a ghost," he muttered, scratching his head.

"Just one's sister." Maya held out a hand. "Maya Corona."

"I see." He shook it. "Gnarlington Gnibblemeister. What brings you out to these parts?"

"We were hoping you could help us find something we need to solve your goblin problem."

"Is that right?" He tweaked his eyeglasses.

"May we come in and talk?"

The gnome nodded and stepped aside, allowing the two to enter. "Make yourselves at home." It was a cozy-looking shack, charmingly rustic, containing not much beyond the necessities. A few maps hung on the walls here and there.

"We appreciate your hospitality," Camden thanked him as he settled by the firepit, shivering a little. Maya instinctively ran a hand over him.

"Think nothing of it." The gnome waved an arm, then pointed. "Cambridge, was it? No, Camelot?"

"Camden," Maya corrected.

"Ah, yes. A good name." He pulled up a stool by the fire and sat. "I'm glad to see you're still out protecting the Fairwoods, even after...what happened."

Cam nodded a little, but said nothing.

"You seem very...normal," Maya told the gnome in an effort to change the subject, taking another look around the cabin. "I feel like everyone else here is competing in some sort of unspoken contest to determine who can be the most insufferably whimsical."

"Whimsy is tiring," Gnarlington shrugged. "It takes too much effort, and gets precious little done."

Maya's brow lifted. Had she at last found the one other reasonable soul in this place? Perhaps he really would have their answer.

Cam's stomach growled. He held an arm to it. "Sorry."

"Ooh." The gnome slipped off his stool. "I've forgotten my manners. Would you two like something to eat?"

Maya glanced at the gryphon, quickly realizing how hungry she was herself. "Yes, please. That would be nice, thank you."

"Come with me out back a moment, then, and help me with the sandwich tree." Gnarlington beckoned, ambling over to his rear door.

"The what...?" Maya followed him through it, stepping out into the yard behind his cabin and up to the tree he indicated. She had hoped it was going to be wedged between two others, or have some kind of pattern of horizontal rings. But, no. From its many branches hung foil-wrapped objects in the shape of Italian rolls. Maya frowned.

"Something wrong?" Gnarlington asked.

"It's just that…a sandwich tree is pretty whimsical."

"It's very *practical*, is what it is. Saves loads on time and the hassle of collecting and storing the individual ingredients. It's sturdy, too." He knocked on it for show. "I uproot it and bring it with me whenever I move. Your sister made it for me, you know." He smiled wistfully, looking it up and down. "She really was something special. I don't know that anyone did more for the Fairwoods than that one girl."

Maya's eyes drifted down to Sofia's ring, and she twisted it around her finger. Her twin had had time for just about everyone, it seemed. Just about.

"Hold this," Gnarlington instructed, handing her the basket sitting under the tree. She obliged, and he propped a ladder against the trunk to climb. Maya held up the basket for him, and he began picking sandwiches. "Looks like we got plenty of ripe ones."

"Cam will probably need a few," Maya suggested. The gnome nodded and kept plunking them in.

When they got back inside, Maya sat down by the gryphon and unwrapped four of them for him, taking one for herself.

"Thanks," Cam said, punctuating it with a nuzzle before digging in. He was becoming less shy with his affections, but she supposed she didn't mind too much.

Maya peeked between the halves of the crisp roll on hers before cutting it in half with her goblin knife. Looked like grilled cheese with peanut butter. It would have to do.

"So," Gnarlington prompted after giving them a few minutes to get something in their stomachs, "I imagine you'd like to get down to business. What is it that I can help you two find?"

"The Gilded Garden," Cam answered, swallowing the last of his third sandwich.

The gnome's brow rose above his spectacles. "Not the most common destination...what makes you want to go there?"

"We need to get the Morning Stone."

"Hm." The geographer rubbed his knees, frowning. "So that's how you mean to deal with the goblins."

Camden fixed the gnome with a determined stare. "It'll be the quickest, safest way to stop them, and make sure they'll never be able to ravage the Fairwoods again."

"A heavy-handed measure, but..." The gnome lifted his shoulders. "You might be right. They were given a chance at peace." He wandered over to a table, pulling out a map and a star chart.

Maya finished her sandwich and stood, stepping over along with Cam to watch.

"Let's see, then." Producing a compass and protractor, the geographer set to work between the two sheets of canvas, every now and then referencing a logbook and scribbling additional notes into it.

Finally, scratching his chin, Gnarlington pointed to a spot on the map with the head of the compass. "The entrance should be here, in Deep Ridge."

Camden's ears and wings drooped. "That...will be a problem."

Maya turned to him. "Why?"

"Deep Ridge is the troll village. They don't let outsiders in."

"Well, we've made it this far." Maya put her hands on her hips, feeling uncharacteristically optimistic. "We'll figure it out." Silly as it was, things seemed to have a way of just working out in this place. As long as she could continue putting up with its incessant quirks, she was fairly certain she could forge ahead, get the stone, do whatever needed doing with it, and make it back home by tomorrow night, just as she'd planned.

Cam regarded her, ears perking, then parted his beak in a hesitant grin before casting his gaze downward.

Maya raised an eyebrow. "What?"

"Nothing. You just...really sounded like her."

Maya sucked in her lips, then looked back to Gnarlington. "Is there anything else we should know?"

The gnome sat down, rubbing at his shoulder. "The entrance will likely be unassuming. Look for something off about the air – the smells and sounds. Once you're in, be mindful of the spirits. Try not to lose your way. Don't stay any longer than you must. The exit can take you anywhere within the Fairwoods; you need only to speak it before you step through."

"Have you been there before?"

"Once." He inclined his head slowly. "Once was enough."

She wasn't sure what to make of that, so she simply nodded in return. "We're grateful for your help, Mr.

Gnibblemeister. And your sandwiches, even if they aren't strictly rational."

Gnarlington offered a mild smile, patting her on the shoulder. "Good luck, Maya Corona. The Fairwoods are in good hands, I think."

"Deep Ridge is back the other way," Cam said as they departed the gnome's cabin. "We can rest up at the den, and plan our approach in the morning."

It was past dark when they made it back to Cam's place, but Maya wasn't feeling particularly tired. Her mind wandered through the events of the last few days, and she reflected on how strange it was, after all these years, to be experiencing the Fairwoods from this perspective. From Sofia's perspective – minus the heroics and magical powers, anyway. What a life her sister had lived. Maya felt wholly out of turn in it, in this adventure that should have been Sofia's to have, yet in this place, with Sofia's ring, with Sofia's gryphon, Maya thought she might feel closer to her sister than she had when she was alive.

"Would you help me with these?" Cam asked, pulling on his bandages. Maya cut them away with her dagger and inspected the wounds beneath, amazed to see how quickly he had recovered. Even the deepest gouges had become little more than scratches. Another advantage of being a perfectly crafted fairytale life-form, she supposed.

When free of the gauze, Camden curled up on his pads and threw a hopeful glance or two her way, trying not to look too expectant.

"O.K., *guapo*," she muttered, slipping over to cuddle up next to him, pretending only to be doing so for his sake. He pulled her closer into his fluffy warmth, and she silently reproached herself for liking it as much as she did. It was not constructive to find such comfort in sentimentality, and allowing herself to do so seemed like a betrayal to her better judgment, to her own identity. But...there was just something so pleasant about this abandonment of practicality, that for once she decided it might be all right to let it slide.

Maybe, the smallest of thoughts whispered, there could be more to her life than being *hueca*.

"What do you think the goblins want?" she asked Camden, turning her mind elsewhere.

"Hmm?" was all she got in return.

"Both times they've attacked, they've demanded I give them something. It's not the ring...so what could it be, do you think? What would I have that they'd be after?"

Cam shifted, silent for a moment. "I don't know. But soon enough, it won't matter. They won't be able to take anything from you or the rest of the Fairwoods again."

"I guess so. I'm just curious...they seem so adamant about it."

He offered only a reassuring nudge in response, and soon she felt him fall asleep.

Turning her ringed hand up before her, she focused on her palm, wondering if curiosity was enough to weave with (and if such pondering would feed into itself). Maybe if she started with something small.

Make a pebble, she told herself, and flexed her fingers. She concentrated hard. Then harder, trying to visualize the tiny rock appearing in her palm. She held her breath and felt herself tense up, her jaw clenching as she attempted to force her will into being.

A small spark of orange energy flitted across her hand.

She almost lurched, but mindful of Camden, kept herself still. There was no pebble, no trace of anything that had changed. But that had been something, hadn't it? She took a deep breath, stretched her wrist, and tried again. This time she put her whole body into it, intent on squeezing the willpower from every inch of herself into this one tiny task.

Make a pebble.

Another ghostly spark puffed briefly into existence.

This was kind of exhausting. Was that one any bigger than the last? It didn't seem like it.

Maya tried a third time, almost groaning with how tight she clenched her gut. Nothing. Then a fourth time. Nothing.

Make a stupid pebble!

She tried again. And again. For what seemed like hours. She had been close, hadn't she? Now she couldn't even get the orange light to reappear.

Finally, she let her arm rest, and leaned back into Cam. There was no reason to be disappointed, she reminded herself. She was not a weaver. Just a stand-in, doing a favor for a fairytale, borrowed from the world where she belonged.

~Part III~

The Cat at the End

Maya awoke alone on the pads to the sound of quiet voices outside. She stood and stretched a little, feeling that she hadn't gotten much sleep. She could deal with it – she'd be in her own bed tonight. And even better, could shower.

She stepped out of the den to see Camden talking to Kallot.

"Morning, Ms. Corona!" the satyr grinned, twirling his flute. "Enjoying your stay with Camden in the Cam-den?"

Maya inclined her head tiredly to hide her grimace. "Hello, Kallot." She scanned the area. "What's going on?"

"Cam here was just giving me the update. Sounds like you two have made a good bit of progress in the last couple days! Not that I should have expected any less from the Heroine's twin sister." He played a few notes on his flute for some reason.

"We're still in a bit of a tricky situation with Deep Ridge," Cam pointed out.

"Maybe. Maybe not." Kallot folded his arms, tapping the flute to his chin. "The trolls are extremely solitary, and don't let outsiders in their midst, it's true. But I do seem to remember Sofia being an exception – she did save their village from the Puce Giant, after all."

Maya tried not to imagine a puce giant. She was unsuccessful.

"She did," Cam confirmed, "but their gratitude wouldn't extend to me or Maya. Sofia was the only one they would have let in."

"Right." Kallot looked to Maya and winked.

Camden's eyes widened, catching his meaning. "That's..." His ears flattened. "That's too dangerous. I can't let her go in by herself."

Maya glanced back and forth between them. "Wait...are you suggesting I pretend to *be* Sofia?"

Cam turned an anxious gaze her way. "You don't have—"

"It's fine," she cut him off, sounding more certain than she felt. She had said they would find a way, and this one, uncomfortable as it might be, seemed like it'd get the job done well enough. Everyone wanted her to be Sofia anyway, right?

"But..." Cam stepped up closer, voice lowering. "You'd have to do it alone."

"I know." She reached up and rubbed his ear.

A rush of air sounded overhead. Maya looked up to see Nissa gliding down toward them, the Maple Witch on her back.

"Your Maplety," Kallot greeted as she landed. "What an unexpected pleasure!" He half-bowed, twirling his flute to one side, then put his free hand to a hip and grinned widely. "I see you've got yourself a pegasus."

"Volequus," Maya corrected, before Nissa could complain. The mare gave her an appreciative nod, which she found herself returning.

"Ah, of course," the satyr smirked.

"Nice to see you as well, Kallot," the witch remarked, perhaps not entirely in earnest, as she slipped off her mount. "I hope everyone is having the loveliest morning."

"What brings you out this way?" Camden asked. Was he hiding behind Maya?

"Oh, you wouldn't believe it, Cammy," the witch laughed. "I seem to have baked far too many maple cakes! But then I thought – you know who might appreciate them?" She produced a cloth sack full of the fragrant pastries, offering them up. "Now that we're all good friends."

Maya thought the excuse dubious; she had seen how the witch 'baked'. Still, the food smelled appetizing. "Thank you. That's very kind." She accepted the sack and pulled one out, wasting no time in biting in.

"Oh, of course." The witch clasped her hands together and smiled. "I also wanted to check in and see how things were going. Have you gotten any further with your weaving?"

"No," Maya said around a cake. It was close enough to true.

The witch pouted a little, but bobbed her head. "Did you track down Gnarlington, at least?"

"Yeah," Maya replied after working down another mouthful. "We're about to go get the stone." She held out a cake for Cam, who eyed it uncertainly, then sent a weak smile in the witch's direction before snapping it up.

"I see." The witch clasped her hands behind her back. "Then I'm just in time to give you this." She reached into somewhere – her gown didn't seem like it would have pockets – and pulled out a clothespeg. "For luck. It once belonged to the Oak Witch, and it's her stone you mean to take."

"Thanks…" Maya wasn't sure what she'd do with a clothespeg, but she accepted it and stuck it in the pocket of her jeans. "Do you know how I'll find the stone, exactly?"

"Once you're in the garden, the ring should lead you to it."

Maya nodded, twisting the ring around her finger.

"Now, how's my little Cammy been holding up?"

As the witch skipped up to tackle the gryphon, Kallot slipped an arm around Maya's shoulders and took her aside.

"Hey, Maya," he said lowly, voice still upbeat but taking on a serious edge. "I know we've got a plan in motion and all that, but something's still sitting dizzy with me about this whole goblin mess."

"What do you mean?"

"Well, the more I see of it, the less sense any of it makes. There's no obvious goal, no intent of conquering. It's sloppy, even for goblins. Just violence. It's almost like they've got some kind of vendetta."

"They keep asking me for something, but I haven't figured out what," she offered, shrugging.

Kallot bit his lower lip, raising an eyebrow. "That right? Huh… Well, I'm gonna check up on a few more leads today, and I'll stop back by here tonight after you've got the stone – assuming everything goes well. So hold off on pulling the trigger until then, mm?"

Maya inclined her head. She wasn't sure she liked the idea of dragging things out longer than they needed to be, but it seemed like a reasonable request when considering the permanence of the solution they meant to implement.

The satyr took her other shoulder and turned her to face him. "And, Maya? Just...be careful, yeah? No telling what you're gonna have to face."

"O.K." She averted her eyes, unsure of what else to say. He let her go, and she made her way over to rescue Camden from the Maple Witch.

"Ready?" the gryphon asked her, his tone half-reluctant for the task ahead and half-grateful for the diversion at present.

"I think so," Maya replied.

"Well," the witch chimed, taking the hint, "I shall wish you the best of luck, then." She returned to Nissa and climbed onto her back. "Do us proud!"

"Are you sure you want to go through with this?" Cam prompted as Kallot and the witch departed. "We could still find another way..."

"It'll be all right," Maya reassured him, thinking that it should be the other way around. "I'll go in, get it, get back, and we'll be done with all this."

Cam nodded, then took a deep breath and gazed off in the other direction. "It's a bit of a ways. I was wondering if maybe..." His jaw twitched.

"What?" Maya crossed her arms and pursed her lips. She had an idea of what was coming.

The gryphon pawed shyly at the grass. "I wondered if you'd like...if maybe you'd want to...to..." He fluffed his wings.

• • •

The flight was exhilarating. Maya was expecting – maybe even kind of hoping – that it would just be nerve-racking and awkward, but the cold rush of air against her, the ripple of Camden's muscles at work below her, and the riotous tingling all throughout her made for an intense experience that she could not bring herself to grudge. The sight of the clear sky all around and the ground far beneath, unobstructed by glass and unfiltered by screen, was nothing short of marvelous.

When they landed on a hill above the village, Maya slipped off the gryphon's back and took a few unsteady steps, shaky but invigorated from the ride. Was this how it was for Sofia every time? Or did being *hueca* just leave that much more room for these sensations to occupy?

"This is it," Cam panted.

"Yeah." Maya looked down at the settlement. It was surrounded by a log-wall, but from the angle of the hill she could see the tops of wooden structures bound with straw. She straightened her clothes, regretting again the loss of the changes she'd brought with her, and glanced back to Cam. "How do I look?"

"Capable," he smiled.

She nodded sharply. "Gnarlington said the exit would take me anywhere, so once I find the stone, I'll come back to your den." As much as she wouldn't have minded another ride, she had to keep some semblance of sensibility intact. "So...I guess I'll see you tonight."

"Maya?"

"Hm?" As she turned around, Camden sat back on his haunches and threw his arms around her, drawing her in tight and encircling her with his wings. The warmth of the embrace drove away the chill from the flight in an instant. His heart was still pounding from the exertion, announcing its raw power in a harsh but soothing rhythm. Maya could only close her eyes and return the hug.

"Come back safe," he whispered.

"I will." She took his face between her hands and kissed him on the forehead, then began her march down the hill toward the village of the trolls.

"What do you want?" one of the spear-toting sentries barked as she neared the gateway through the wall. He and his companion were tall, furry creatures, colored a mottled, pukey greenish-brown. Their features were somewhat apish, somewhat reptilian, their clothing tanned hide with weaves of brightly-dyed straw jutting here or hanging there in what could equally have been a status symbol or fashion statement.

Maya cleared her throat and stood up straight. "I need to come in."

"*No outsiders!*" the sentry roared, moistening her face. She blinked and scrunched it up.

"But—"

"Go away!"

"Hold on," the other sentry grunted, jabbing his companion with an elbow. "I think I recognize her."

"Huh?" The first sentry looked dubiously at the other.

"Yeah." The second squinted at Maya, then his eyes widened. "Whoa, yeah, this is—this is the Heroine of the Fairwoods."

"Wait, really? The one who saved Deep Ridge from the Puce Giant? Nuh-uh."

"You were still in training, but I was there. I'm telling you, this is her! This is Sofia."

"Yes," Maya agreed, holding up her hand to show off the ring. "I am *exactly* Sofia."

"She's a weaver," the second sentry warned out of the side of his mouth. "She could probably turn us into bacon with that ring. Crisp, delicious bacon."

The first sentry considered this, then regarded her cautiously. "And...you want to come into our village?"

Maya put her hands on her hips, narrowed her eyes, and nodded gravely.

"Why?" the sentry frowned.

What would Sofia say? "Important...time-sensitive... Heroine business." That was probably not at all what Sofia would have said. Maybe this wouldn't be quite as easy as she imagined.

The sentries looked at each other. "Sounds serious," the second nodded. "All right. I'll take you to the chief."

Then again, maybe trolls had a few things in common with goblins.

"Hold the gate for a few," the second sentry told the first, then escorted Maya into the settlement.

It was a pretty populous, bustling place, she could see from the inside. Nothing obvious stood out to explain the xenophobia, but she did get a number of strange glances as she wandered through – some distrustful, some worried, some just surprised. Many were clutching anxiously at their caps. In fact, she noticed every troll in here was wearing some garish variety of hat. Some of them more than one.

"Chief Gurhteg," the sentry called to an overdressed troll talking to a few soldier-looking types in front of one of the larger buildings.

The chief turned. Upon his head rested at least five different hats, stacked in a gaudy, off-kilter tower of unflattering colors in haphazard arrangement. He scanned for his addresser, blinking when he saw Maya. "Sofia...?" He waved away the sentry, who pounded his chest twice before setting off to return to his post. "What brings you back to Deep Ridge? Not that it isn't always nice to see you, but...is something wrong?"

"It's nice to see you again too, Chief Gurhteg." Maya curtseyed. It was a bad curtsey. Would Sofia have curtseyed? The chief's raised eyebrow said probably not. "Things are all right for the time being, but—"

"Then where's your hat?" the chief frowned, the feathered burgundy tricorne at his apex wobbling.

"My hat?"

"Your hat. You're not wearing it." He folded his arms, lips curling in displeasure.

Maya froze. This was not exactly the type of complication she had expected to encounter. "My hat," she repeated dumbly.

"Your hat! The beautiful stovepipe I gave you for helping us with that giant business." His eyes narrowed. "You didn't tell anyone where you got it, did you?" His nostrils flared. "You didn't *sell* it, did you?"

That hideous thing at Cam's place, she realized. She set her hand awkwardly upon Gurhteg's arm, and tried to put on a convincing Sofia. "Oh, I would never do that. It's safely back...home, with its...spikes and its," she twirled her finger in the air, "...swirls. I didn't want to mess it up by, you know, *adventuring* in it."

The chief continued to stare for an uncomfortable few seconds. "Hmm. I guess it *is* for the best not to be parading it around out there for all to covet." He seemed to relax a little, but then grew skeptical. "But that gift was a one-time thing, you understand. I hope you have not become so enamored with it that you've come back intending to steal away the rest of our hats when we're not looking."

Maya felt her mind trip over itself as it tried to render a response to that particular concern. "N-no. I—no."

"Are you sure? I could hardly blame you. Troll hats are the very best sort of hat – undoubtedly the envy of all other races." He adjusted his third cap, a boxy pink-streaked beige affair.

"I'm sure." She squinted slightly, turning her head a few degrees. "Is hat burglary a common problem for you?"

"Of course not," Gurhteg sneered. "Do you think we're foolish enough to let anyone else come in here and ogle them? Just look at their splendor, their magnificence; the desire to snatch up such fine headwear would be far too enticing."

Maya took another glance around the village, and found herself utterly untempted to pilfer any article of clothing from its residents. "They're...certainly something."

"Then you understand why we must be stern." He bobbed his head stiffly, somehow maintaining the integrity of his motley steeple. "So as much as you must want another for yourself, know that I will not tolerate sticky fingers, from the Heroine or otherwise."

Maya sucked in her lips, reminding herself that protesting this peculiar paranoia was not the reason she was here. She really should have learned by now to take these things in stride... "Fair enough. In any case, I've only come here to find something."

"Find what, exactly?" He wrinkled his nose, still leering suspiciously.

She didn't know of any reason not to tell the truth, she supposed. Well, about this, anyway. "The entrance to the Gilded Garden. Do you happen to know where it is?"

The chief's eyes widened a little. "No...but you think it's here, do you? Interesting." He rubbed his chin.

"Gnarlington Gni—the gnome does."

"I suppose he would know."

"Yes. Well, I need to go there to stop the goblins from terrorizing the rest of the Fairwoods."

"Goblins," one of the soldiers spat. "Caught one of those hatless pests snooping around Deep Ridge the other day. Scared 'im off, though."

"More like you let him get away," another soldier needled.

"Shut up," growled the first.

Gurhteg eyed them reproachfully, and to Maya said, "Who am I to stand in your way, then?" He gestured to the pair of soldiers. "My men will be glad to assist with your search and help you...stay on track." He tapped the grey-and-yellow splotched beret at the base of his stack and winked.

The soldiers double-pounded their chests and stepped up to Maya. She had the distinct impression that this was not an offer she could refuse.

"The Fairwoods thank you, Chief," she intoned, then set off with her escort in tow.

She had no idea what she was doing. That fact did not take her long to realize, but she did her best to put on a show. She found she could look competent if she simply kept up a slightly annoyed expression, paused often to look left and right, knelt down on occasion to scoop up and investigate the dirt with her dagger, and said "hmm" a lot.

She was supposed to be looking for something out of place, something that didn't belong, but as far as she could tell, she was the only thing here that fit that description. It wasn't the easiest task to notice something different about a place she'd never seen before.

"Is this something?" the soldier in the cyan toque asked, pointing with a large, untrimmed toe-claw. Maya decided to think of that one as Bigsy, because he was slightly taller than the other one. She could have just as easily asked him what his name was, but she couldn't really bring herself to care.

She glanced down where he indicated. "That's a rock," she sighed.

"Yeah, but it has a crack in it."

"I don't think anyone's going to be able to fit through a three-inch crack."

The troll shrugged. "Just trying to help."

"Can't you weave something that'll find the entrance?" the other soldier inquired, his chartreuse slouch angled over one eye. He was Snortsy, because he kept sniffling. Maybe he had a cold.

"Weaving doesn't work that way," Maya quickly dismissed, although she wondered if it really would be that easy. Then she stopped. "Wait. Do you hear that?"

"Huh?" Bigsy looked around.

"Our voices. Listen." The resonance was wrong. "They're flat." The subtle reverberations which had followed them throughout the rest of their march were missing. She was by no means an expert on acoustics, but she couldn't see anything about this spot that she thought would change the sound properties. "Doesn't that seem strange?"

The trolls glanced at each other and shrugged.

Maya paced around the area, a large patch of grass and trees between the log-wall and a worn dirt path. She took a couple steps at a time, stopping between them to sing an A-note (she knew it was an A-note because of an old tuning fork she used to smack and rest on everything to see what she could make ring).

As she followed the dampening effect, she began to smell what might have been rain. She looked up – the sky was still clear. She tried to narrow in on the scent, and where it grew mildly stronger, she heard a faint rippling, sort of staticky noise. She stood still, panning her head around.

"Did you find it?" Snortsy inquired, sniffing. His tone was growing bored.

She held up a finger to hush him, and continued to look and listen.

There were two trees, she noticed, that grew only a few feet apart, and two of their thick branches touched overhead, forming a conspicuous sort of archway. She walked over and took a circuit around them, studying them closely for anything out of the ordinary. Nothing seemed to stand out, but still, she had a hunch. She took a few steps back, picked up a stone, and rolled it between the trees. It settled unspectacularly on the other side.

"I thought rocks weren't going to help," Bigsy complained.

"I guess they won't," Maya muttered, walking disappointedly past the trees to see what else might be of interest. She had been sure there was something about that tree-gate, but apparently her instincts weren't cut out for this. She pursed her lips and took one more peek back.

The stone was not there.

She stared for a moment at where it should have been, then went back around. She could still see it when she looked between the trunks, but if she peered around them, it was gone.

"Ah-ha," she couldn't help but whisper. She crept up to the trees and slowly, tentatively, stuck an arm through. It felt slightly cool, but nothing changed visually. She took a long breath, steadying herself, then stepped fully through the threshold.

The scenery before her faded into something else. The stone she had tossed was at her feet, but around it was much lusher, more vivid grass. The troll civilization was gone, replaced with densely packed trees and bushes extending all around her as far as she could see, parting in a number of paths that led further in. The sky was a far richer blue, vibrant fruits dangled invitingly in all directions, and everything gleamed with a golden luster when the light hit it right.

Maya turned back at the sound of the trolls; they followed her through, gaping as they took it all in. From this end, the gate was a perfect arch, ornately carved of white-and-silver marble, and much like on the other side, looking through it revealed nothing extraordinary. The trolls hesitated by the sides of the gate, eyeing each other, and Maya realized that their gazes spoke more of trepidation than admiration.

"We'll stay here and guard the exit," Snortsy suggested, fidgeting with the handle of his curved sword.

"Yeah," Bigsy agreed fervently, bobbing his head. "Wouldn't want anything sneaking through into Deep Ridge. Hurry and do what you need to do."

Maya raised an eyebrow, but didn't really mind. It was not as if they were of much use to begin with. Picking a path at random, she set off into the depths of the Gilded Garden.

It should have been serene, this casual stroll through this resplendent orchard, but there were things Maya began to notice that made her eager to get it over with.

The air, while fragrant, was somehow stale. It possessed the same echoless quality that had led her to the gate. There was no trace of the gentle breeze which was ever-present throughout the village. She could hear birds singing their peaceful melodies overhead, but even their voices felt empty, and as hard as she studied the canopy above, she could not actually *see* any birds at all. The garden was lit brightly, as if by noon sunlight, but no sun shone in that perfectly clear sky. No shadows stretched along the ground.

Maya focused on Sofia's ring. It was supposed to lead her to the Morning Stone. If she concentrated enough, she thought she could feel a subconscious pull in one direction or another, and she tried to use that feeling to guide her through the branching paths amidst the trees. At every turn, she used the goblin knife to score the ground in the direction from which she came; she wasn't about to get herself lost in here.

She had likely been wandering for half an hour when she came upon a dead end. She glared disapprovingly at the ring and prepared to turn back, but a rising sound gave her pause. It was like a chorus of exhaling. No, *moaning*.

To either side of her, the trees were taking on broad, black, jagged mouths, slowly opening wider as the sound increased in volume.

Ahead in her path, a pool of inky darkness began to ooze out of the ground, wafting upward and taking shape as the light seeped from the empty sky. Maya simply stared at it, unsure of what to do. Maybe it was something she would have to face in order to get the stone.

In another moment, the darkness coalesced into a wraith-like shape. It stood still, four plumes of black flame flickering above its shoulders, eyeless but staring right at Maya.

"You don't belong here," one of the tree-mouths rasped as the others continued to moan.

"I know," Maya sighed, turning the ring around her finger.

"Go back while you can," another tree-mouth groaned.

"I can't yet. I need to get something."

"You mean to rob us," a tree-mouth hissed.

Maya squinted. "I guess..." No one had really implied that taking the stone was not O.K.

One of the wraith's floating flames turned green for a moment, and the sound of a baby's laugh in reverse came from nowhere.

Another tree-mouth asked, "Do you think you can do better than us?"

"I don't know what you mean."

"Do you think creation is simple? That it comes without cost?"

Maya shook her head. "I'm no good at creating anything."

The wraith floated a little closer. Another of its flames flashed blue, accompanied by a distorted eagle's screech.

"Control is no less perilous," warned a tree.

"I'll be careful," Maya promised.

A flame blinked red, sounding the broken peal of a bell. "Do you believe that is enough? Do you think you can anticipate every outcome? Comprehend every conse-quence?"

There was such ire in that tone, such personal bitterness. Maya thought she might know who she was talking to. "You're the spirit of the Oak Witch, aren't you?"

For several seconds, there was no response. Then, the sky re-lightened, the tree-mouths closed into nothing, and the shadows making up the wraith dissolved to reveal a simple-featured woman with skin of wood and hair of leaves.

A hamadryad.

"Perceptive," the witch consented. "But that hardly makes you worthy of the Morning Stone."

"I don't really mean to be worthy of anything. I'm just trying to help save the Fairwoods from the goblins so I can go back home."

"If you ever want to see your home again, you had best turn back now."

Maya frowned, taking a look around the garden. "What about the homes of everyone here? Don't you want them taken care of? I mean, you made this whole place, didn't you?"

The dryad looked her over with her solid black eyes. "I did. And I paid dearly for it." She gestured mildly around herself. "I wanted to create a perfect world. One with order and structure. One free from strife. But...life has a way of outgrowing any pattern. The more complex my children and their world became, the harder it was to hold them in line. They began to defy my design." She clasped her wooden hands together. "It grew difficult to manage them alone, so I created more powerful beings to keep them in check, and when they in turn resisted me, I wove those more powerful still. Before I realized it, my creations had surpassed me. And they wanted their freedom. So they took it." She stepped toward Maya. "They rose against me, found my body, and chopped it down."

"They killed you?"

The witch nodded. "All I wanted was to offer them a peaceful existence. To give them purpose..." She spread her hands. "Life craves purpose."

Maya twisted up her mouth. "Well...I'm sorry things didn't work out for you, but I still need to borrow your stone." She stuck her hands in her pockets and felt something – the clothespeg. What would a dryad need a clothespeg for, anyway?

The witch tilted her head. "Would you wish for a fate such as mine?"

"No, but…" Maya sighed, fidgeting with the peg. It must have been *part* of the Oak Witch, she suddenly realized. Made from her true body.

When you possess a part of someone…

Maya pulled out the peg and held it up before the witch. "But I think you need to let me through." She squinted. "Right?"

The dryad's brow lifted slightly as her eyes focused on the peg. "Consider your path prudently, Maya Corona." She evaporated into a cloud of black smoke, and the trees behind her began rearranging themselves to form a new route.

Maya breathed deeply, and continued onward.

And then, there it was. Another ten minutes of walking brought her to the end of the trail, where a massive oak stump sat, and floating above it, a chunk of lambent amber the size of her fist.

Lying beside the stump, unexpectedly, was a small green-eyed black cat, idly swishing its tail as it watched her approach. The only other presumably living thing she had seen in this place. Probably some strange kind of final guardian. Certainly nothing to do with any silly Fairwoods idioms.

"I suppose you must be the Cantankerous Cat or some such," Maya ventured.

"Not really," the cat responded, sitting up.

"Well, whoever you are, I'm here for the stone."

"Is that so?"

"It is." Maya twisted the ring around her finger, waiting for something weird to happen.

A few moments passed, and nothing did. The cat looked casually from Maya to the stone, and then back. "Do you intend to take it, then…?"

"Yes." She furrowed her brow. "Is that all right?"

"You are asking me?"

"Well, yes. Can I take it? I'm sure someone will bring it back when we're done."

The cat stared at her for several seconds, then regarded the stone again. "I shall not stop you."

"Thank you," Maya nodded, then stepped cautiously up onto the stump. That seemed a little too easy.

The ring, which was already humming, began to vibrate as she reached for the lump of resin. The sensation grew arm-numbing as she poised her hand underneath it. Both ring and stone were glowing, yearning for each other, ready to meet. Bracing herself for the impending spectacle, Maya planted her feet, reached up, and grabbed ahold of the Morning Stone.

The glowing and shaking stopped, and her prize went unremarkably along with her.

"Hm," the cat voiced. "After all that, I admit I expected something a little more eventful."

Maya stared at the thing in her grasp, then raised an eyebrow at him. "What do you mean? Haven't others taken it before?"

"I have not the slightest idea," the cat replied, glancing around the area. "I merely wandered in here for a moment or two of peace. It is a rather tranquil place, would you not agree?"

Maya pursed her lips. "You could have said that *before* I almost got my arm blown off."

The cat regarded her with a hint of amusement, then lay back down. "Curious how a modest thing like proximity can convey the impression of authority, is it not?"

Sighing wearily, stone in hand, Maya stepped off the stump and began her trek back toward the entrance.

Tranquil was maybe not the word she would have used to describe the Gilded Garden. There wasn't much about it that put her at ease. She was feeling pretty tired, though, now that her quest was essentially over. Very tired, actually.

Stopping along the path where she had encountered the Oak Witch, she sat down with her back against a tree (she made sure to check for a mouth) to rest for a moment, feeling her eyelids already drooping. She really shouldn't have stayed up so late trying to make that pathetic pebble. She'd been able to do this whole thing without once needing to weave.

"You—you might not wanna do that," warned a tentative voice, drawing her back from her diminishing consciousness.

Maya looked up and saw a goblin standing a few feet beside her.

Rising quickly, she fumbled for her dagger and held it at the ready toward him.

"Whoa, hey!" The goblin took a step back and held up his hands, then his eyes grew large as he looked her up and down. "Sofia?" He smiled, almost giddily. "Sofia! Hey, hey—look, I'm not gonna pick a fight; I know what you could do to me." He glanced nervously at the goblin blade and held his hands up higher to accentuate the point.

Maya narrowed her eyes, but put the dagger back through her belt. "At least one of you has some sense," she said, trying to sound confident.

"Yes, ma'am," the goblin replied, then saluted. "Lieutenant Tellock, First Officer of the Fourteenth Regiment in service to His Royal Highness the Goblin Prince." He was a little snappier than the average goblin, clad in a black leather vest, trunks, and bracer-cuffs. He looked even more exhausted than she was, though.

He cleared his throat, posture loosening, and rubbed at his shoulder. "I—I know you didn't do it, Ms. Heroine. A lot of us still believe in you – please know that."

"Didn't do what, exactly?"

"You know…steal the Goblin Prince's belt."

"His *belt*?"

"Yeah. The royal belt. The dark one with the golden wheels and topazes? The thing that signifies his right to rule the goblin kingdom."

"*That's* what they think I have?"

"Yes, ma'am. Some of the fourth and the seventh swear they saw you make off with it, but I don't believe that for a second. Unfortunately…the prince did. But I haven't forgotten what you did for us. You saved us, you freed us – why do that only to turn around and insult us?" He shook his head. "I know our Heroine wouldn't do that."

Would she? It certainly didn't sound like anything Sofia would do. "When do they say sh—I did this?"

"Uh…'bout a month ago, now."

Maya scrunched up her face. Sofia could not very well have done such a thing several months after getting herself killed. She would have to see what Kallot thought about all this. "What are you doing in the Gilded Garden, anyway?"

"Oh, well, I came here to ask the spirits for help. To guide us to the truth. To show us how to set things right without more bloodshed." He scratched the back of his neck. "And, uh, heh – here I am getting a chance to talk to you yourself."

"How'd you get past the trolls?"

"Fourteenth Regiment is a stealth squad, ma'am." He grinned proudly. "Getting in was the easy part though. I, um…it's getting out that I can't seem to manage. I don't think it…well, um—I don't think it *likes* it when anyone leaves."

"You can follow me if you want, then," Maya offered, feeling a little pleased with herself. "I marked the way back toward the entrance."

Tellock looked uncertain, but inclined his head and stepped up beside her. As they began walking, he saw what she was holding and asked, "Is that—you got the Morning Stone?"

She looked down at it, now a little uncomfortable about its purpose. "Yeah."

"Wow. That's great! I came across it a bit ago, but couldn't even pick it up. You're gonna use it to fix everything, huh? I knew it! We can put a stop to all this fighting."

Maya swallowed. She was so close to being done with this whole thing. Why did it have to get more complicated at the last second?

They marched on, following the scores in the ground, until by Maya's count they would be approaching the entrance at the next turn. "Just about there," she informed, and yawned.

When they rounded the final corner, however, the gate was not in sight. As she continued forward, Maya saw that the clearing where it stood was not even there. Only another branching path.

"What...?" Maya frowned, looking for a score mark in each new direction, but finding none. "It should...it was right here."

Tellock sighed, squatting. "It doesn't want to let us go. This is what I was talking about."

"Lame," Maya groaned, closing her eyes and squeezing the stone.

"Had a feeling I might never get out of here..."

"Well...stop it." Maybe this was one of those things where the paths looped impossibly back on themselves, but the exit could be found if navigating them in a certain order. That's how it worked in video games, anyway.

Maya transferred the stone to her other hand and held up the one wearing the ring. She concentrated, seeing if it would guide her toward the exit, but it only seemed to be pulling toward the hand at her side. "Hrm."

Then she held up the stone instead and focused on it. She could feel a drawing sensation with it, too, but it was back in the direction they'd come from, toward the oak stump.

Maya ground her teeth, but then had an idea. "This way," she beckoned to the goblin, and set off in the direction opposite of the way it wanted her to go.

She took the diminishing strength of the stone's pull as a good sign, and sure enough, after a few more turns, they came upon the marble arch of the gate.

Beside it, she saw Bigsy kneeling over Snortsy's unconscious form.

Bigsy snapped his head around at the sound of Maya's approach. "He won't wake up. He won't wake up!" He looked on the verge of panic.

"What happened?" Maya asked.

"He just fell asl—*you!*" He stood and drew his curved sword, leveling it at Tellock. "You're the trespasser!" His eyes darted back to Maya. "What are you doing with him?"

Maya held up her hands in a placating gesture. "I just— he was—look, it doesn't matter."

"I don't want any trouble," Tellock assured, but there was an edge to his voice.

The troll snarled, slashing his sword in the air. "Liar! You wanted to make off with all our best hats!" He slashed the sword again, then glared at Maya. "Get rid of him." He pointed his sword to Snortsy. "And fix him, before his hat gets stolen!"

"Nobody wants your *stupid hats*!" the goblin growled.

"Shut up!" Bigsy pulled nervously at his tunic with his free hand, head darting about the area, then stomped his foot and pointed to his companion again. *"Fix him, now!"*

Maya blinked. "What do you expect me to do?"

"You're a weaver! Make water, or a bell, or hartshorn salt, or *something!*"

"I..." Maya clutched at the ring, fumbling for an excuse.

"FIX HIM!" The troll's chest was heaving, his mouth foaming. He was definitely losing his head.

Tellock put a hand on Maya's shoulder, stepping protectively around her and palming the hilt of his own short sword. "You can't talk to the Heroine that way."

"Get away from her!" Bigsy swung his sword, and the goblin quickly pulled them both back out of its arc.

"Stop!" Maya waved her hands at the troll. "I'll fix him."

The troll stared, eyes wide and nostrils flaring, but let her slowly sidestep over to Snortsy's body.

Stalling for time, Maya knelt down and felt the troll's neck. He had a sluggish pulse, and he was breathing. She shook him, slapped him, pinched his nose. No good. She rose and looked him up and down, then held the Morning Stone over his form.

Wake up, she commanded.

The command was not heeded. She didn't know why she expected it to be.

"You're not *doing anything!*" Bigsy protested, stomping.

"I'm trying..." She continued to hold the stone over Snortsy, squeezing it and willing it to do something, but it remained a futile effort.

The troll's glare shot between Maya and Tellock, and his face began to twist up in horror. "I saw the Heroine take down a giant. I saw her heal a dozen trolls of their wounds. You can't even wake one up. You—you're an imposter!"

Maya's gut clenched. "No, I just—"

"*A hatless imposter in league with the goblins!*" He lashed a hand out at Maya, and she instinctively brought her arm up to block, gasping as his claws tore through her shirt and flesh and sent her sprawling to the ground.

She rolled onto her back in time to see the troll standing over her, sword poised high and hurtling downward to cleave her in two.

Time seemed to slow down. She was aware of dropping the Morning Stone and holding her ringed hand up before her. In this desperate moment of life-or-death, she channeled every ounce of thought into the ring to manifest a shield, a blast, a sword of her own – anything to change the fate she was about to suffer. Her concentration narrowed, her will focused to a pinpoint, she visualized her salvation, and...

Nope. Not even to save her own life. The blade fell toward her unimpeded.

But it clanged against Tellock's an inch from her body as the goblin dove in between them.

Maya scrambled back and out of the way as Tellock courageously held off the larger creature's sword. As soon as she was clear, the goblin rolled to a stand and swung at Bigsy, but the troll easily parried and slashed back with a crazed fury, harrying him several steps backward until one powerful slice snapped the goblin's sword in half.

Tellock's jaw had an instant to drop before the troll drove his blade through his foe's belly. The poor goblin screamed as Bigsy lifted him off the ground with the sword and held him up to his face.

"I've caught you now, you filthy little sneak," the troll spat.

Tellock managed a pitiful growl in response. Then, with surprising speed, he grabbed the band of the troll's hat and pulled himself in closer; in the same moment, he flicked back his free wrist, causing a small blade to spring forth from his cuff, and jammed it into Bigsy's throat.

The troll gurgled and dropped the goblin, stumbling backward, grasping at his neck. His eyes rolled back, he swayed unsteadily, then toppled, dead.

Maya rushed over to Tellock as he pulled the troll's sword from his abdomen, coughing and groaning. She gingerly helped him lay down on his back and knelt beside him, staring hopelessly at his injury. She had no delusions about his survival.

"That was...very brave," she said quietly, taking his hand.

The goblin smiled weakly, squeezing back. "Coming from you, that means a lot." His eyes were beginning to lose focus. "I had a feeling I wasn't gonna get out of here." He laughed a little, then closed his eyes. "Thank you. Thank you for everything you've done...for all of us. I'm...I'm glad I got to meet you, Sofia."

"Maya," she whispered, but he was gone. She sat still for several moments, staring at his broken blade. Withdrawing her dagger, she placed it on his chest and wrapped his hands around it. Then, dizziness and exhaustion engulfing her, she collapsed onto the grass next to him.

Maybe it was a peaceful place after all, this Gilded Garden. The stillness, the quiet, the softness of the ground. It felt so good just to lie down.

You can stay here if you want.

Perhaps she would. Would that be so bad? She didn't know what she would do if she went back. She hadn't done a single useful thing the entire time she had been in the Fairwoods. She couldn't weave even in the moment of truth. She had come here on a mission to exile an entire race, only to have one of its members sacrifice himself to save her life when she couldn't be bothered to do so herself.

Rest. Forget your troubles.

The grass caressed her and the sunless sunlight washed over her like a golden blanket. The thought of moving became less and less appealing. She was never meant to come to the Fairwoods, she knew. They would not miss her. She was never meant for any of this. Never meant to be a Heroine.

Nothing is expected of you here. There is no pressure, no stress. Only peace.

She thought of Sofia. Sofia had done so much for this place. What right did Maya have to walk around in her stead? Even back at home, she could never hope to fill the void Sofia left in the lives of their family or friends.

There is nothing left for you out there.

But then she thought of Camden. His warm embrace, his soft voice. His anxious eyes pleading for her safety. She had promised him that she would return, hadn't she? And he would be so heartbroken if she didn't...

You needn't worry about anyone else.

He had already lost Sofia. What would losing her do to him? He would be alone. That was such an awful thought... Would he blame himself for letting her come to the garden without him? Would the rest of the Fairwoods blame him for failing to deliver their salvation?

It doesn't matter. Nothing matters anymore.

No. With tremendous effort, Maya rolled to the elbow of her uninjured arm. The wash of vertigo was almost unbearable, but she held fast and did not drop back down.

Stay. Stay here... Stay where everything is simple...

Her body railed at her, resisting every motion, but slowly, painfully, she got to her knees.

It's too much. It's too hard. It's not worth it.

It was. She had to believe it was.

With one final push, one more silent scream, Maya stood up. She kept still for several minutes, fighting to keep her balance, and when at last she dared, she scooped up the Morning Stone and stumbled over to the gate.

"Camden's den," she told it, and stepped through.

It was already evening, and the den was dark as Maya shambled into it. She reached up, feeling for the hanging rock, and banged it with her knuckles, sending a shooting pain down her injured arm. The soft glow filled her vision, and she examined her torn sleeve and the gouges beneath it, realizing they would need tending.

Cam had not yet returned, or had otherwise stepped out, so Maya drug herself over to the desk in the back to find the gauze and balm. She set the Morning Stone on top of it and braced herself against its edge as a wave of dizziness swept through her.

She had done it, she realized, gazing almost incredulously at the chunk of amber. She had completed the quest the Fairwoods put to her and made it back safely. Without weaving, without whimsy, she had actually done it. That fact was as strange as anything else in this place. The issue of the goblins still remained, but she would give Kallot the stone and tell him what she learned, and he could make his own decisions. The only thing she had left to take care of was herself. She opened the top drawer of the desk.

Inside of it, she saw a belt. A dark brown belt with golden wheels and little blue topazes.

For a moment she was certain it was just a fatigue-induced hallucination. But slowly, she reached in and touched it, and her hand told her eyes they were not mistaken.

What did it mean? Why did Cam have the Goblin Prince's belt? The very reason for their attack. Had he found whoever stole it? Then, why hadn't he given it back?

Or, did *he*…? The goblins said they saw Sofia make off with it, but had they just conflated him with her?

What reason would he have? It didn't make any sense. She turned the belt over, racking her mind, and saw something else below it.

A necklace.

A silver leaf necklace.

Sofia's silver leaf necklace.

A necklace she had worn to the lake on that night. Her last night.

Maya fumbled at its duplicate around her neck, making sure it was still there. Her mind fought back against her, refusing to acknowledge what she was seeing. Cam said he had last seen Sofia a week before the accident, had not been back to the lake since. Why would he lie? Nothing about any of this added up.

She continued to stare, dizziness growing, and barely noticed the sound of someone else entering the den.

"Maya!" Cam's voice rang out, excited and relieved. "You're back! And—and you got it... You really got it. That's...you're amazing." She heard a soft thud. "I, um, are you hungry? I got us some dinner. Do you—"

"Camden," Maya interjected, her voice quiet but carrying. He must have sensed something in her tone, for he immediately fell silent. Maya took a lengthy breath, acutely aware of the dull rattling of every nerve, and did not turn around as she continued. "Why do you have Sofia's necklace?"

For a long time, he said nothing. She could hear him breathing, scratching lightly at the ground, his wings rustling against his back. "I..." he finally managed, then swallowed. "I did something very bad, Maya." His tone was shaky, fearful.

Hers was even, weary. "What did you do, Camden?"

"I, um..." He swallowed again. "I was...I was with her...the night when..."

"When she died."

"She..." He took a tremulous breath, pausing for several moments. His voice grew resigned, deflated. "You have to understand, Maya... Sofia was everything to me. My creator, my teacher, my guardian, my friend. I existed for her and her alone. I was her protector, her companion, anything she needed from me. Adventuring with her, defending the Fairwoods from evil, revered as heroes…it was the greatest life anyone could ask for. I would have been content to stay like that forever. But…then we defeated the Cedar Witch."

Maya kept still, gazing at the back wall, just focusing on his voice. His sweet, soft, sad voice.

"I was made for a purpose. But I was also given freedom. And I learned the hard way that those two things cannot coexist. When Sofia began spending less time here…less time with me… I know she had her own life to live in her own world, and she thought she was giving me the same, but making me understand freedom was only opening my eyes to something I could never have. I was bound to her. I *needed* her. I—I could never truly be free while my purpose to my creator still stood."

A swell of nausea poured through Maya, and she gripped tightly at the edge of the desk. "What did you do?" she repeated.

Cam let out a long, unsteady sigh. "I tried to find another way. Please believe I did everything I could to find *any* other way. But I was losing my very reason for existing. And that feeling, Maya… It's like…being trapped in darkness, alone and scared, knowing the one who promised to take care of you is just beyond it, just on the edge, and—and you're screaming and crying for her until your throat is raw and bloody but she won't answer, she won't come. You keep calling and hoping and begging but she'll never come." His voice caught for a moment. "I tried. I tried *so* hard to bear it, but I wasn't strong enough. The only way to stop the pain, the only way to free myself was to...to end my purpose."

"To end Sofia," Maya said. It seemed surreal, as if the words had come from someone else.

"I met her by the lake. Her favorite spot. And I told her...I told her what I'm telling you. She didn't say anything... She just...she looked at me, sad and afraid, but she—she barely fought back when I...when I grabbed her...and I pulled her under the water...and—and I held her there until she stopped struggling." He took another shaky breath. "Her necklace came off in the lake, and I...I needed something to remind me of what I'd done. Of what my selfishness cost."

"So you killed her." There was a sensation building inside Maya stronger than anything she had experienced before. She felt it like a burning, a trembling, a stinging. She *felt*. "You killed the one who gave you life. Who gave you all her time and affection. Who gave you everything. A twelve-year-old girl who loved you more than anything else in either of our worlds, and you *killed* her."

"I..." He made a low, plaintive noise. "She loved you too, Maya. I didn't understand the full extent of my purpose until after she was gone. She didn't just create me as a companion for herself, but...but to look after you if anything happened to her." She heard him take a step forward. "And now you have the ring...and I can still feel the bond."

Maya's eyes widened at the wall, and a chill trickled down her back. "You're going to kill me too." She reached numbly for the dagger that she no longer had.

"I'm sorry... I know that can't possibly mean anything to you now, but I am *so sorry...*" He took another step forward.

She understood what she was feeling. It was anger. It was hate. She had always thought that hate would be straightforward, that it would be the opposite of love, but she realized now that love was its source. The mass to its gravity. She was only capable of feeling this hatred because she had loved Sofia.

Because she loved Camden.

The bitterness of the betrayal roiled inside her, but the weight of the hopelessness, impotency, and fatigue kept her voice listless as she looked down at the goblin's belt. "Why all the run-around? Why provoke the goblins only to keep saving me from them? Why not just do it that night outside my house?"

"Whatever differences you and Sofia had, I—I knew that you couldn't refuse to help us if we were in real trouble, and I needed the Morning Stone to make sure that—that it ends here. The ring could pass on to someone else after you, but if the stone takes its place as my anchor before it has the chance, then...I'll just be like every other Fairwoods native. I'll really be free."

So everything she'd been through had all been a ruse, set up for this singular pursuit. How many had pointlessly died because of it? For what did Tellock just lay down his life? Sadness, fury, pity, and exhaustion warred within Maya, readily filling the empty vessel she had been. She contemplated her encroaching end with a reproachful detachment. What would Sofia think if she could see her here like this? What would she expect from her?

Cam took one more step. She could feel him behind her. "I wish I had the courage to ask for your forgiveness," he murmured, "but I know I don't deserve it. I've been an awful friend. An awful everything... But I want you to know that these past few days with you were a blessing I'll never forget. I've loved you both more than I could ever say; I'm...I'm just too weak to prove it. And I'm too weak to think about what I have to do any longer." He gulped hard, and she felt a great exhalation on her neck. Another eternal second passed, and he asked, "Are you ready?"

Was she ready? Was she prepared to die as her sister had? To leave everyone and everything behind, as she so nearly did in the Gilded Garden? Was there any reason not to, now? She feared she knew the answer. Maya sighed, and closed her eyes. *"Por mi hermana,"* she whispered.

Then she whirled around, wove a knife, and plunged it into Camden's chest.

His cry of shock and pain was quickly constricted to a wheezing rasp. He grasped her shoulder in his talons for support, and gazed at her with drooping ears, a parted beak, and wide, trembling eyes.

Maya looked down at the knife in her hand, scarcely believing what she had done. It wasn't fully formed, only glittering orange energy in a silhouette of the goblin dagger, but it was solid – enough that she could feel the irregular tremors of the gryphon's heart as it struggled desperately to keep beating around the blade.

That perfect heart Sofia had so lovingly crafted, and Maya was ruining it. Destroying this beautiful creature that was her sister's only living legacy. The cub she had once cradled in her arms, his hot blood now flowing down the one she was killing him with. She thought she could feel his life force draining, seeping helplessly back into the ring that had lent it to him. He would not recover from this. She could not take it back.

"Maya..." he croaked. His breathing was wet and labored. "I..." His eyes bored into her, full of fear and sorrow. Tears dripped steadily down from them, and Maya was alarmed to realize that her own were mirroring the act.

The flames of her hate and anger were rapidly dwindling, and in their place arose an emotion far more unpleasant.

Grief.

Grief for Camden, for Sofia, even for Tellock and the rest of his race. It was all catching up to her in a flood of uncompromising *feeling*. Was this what it truly meant not to be *hueca*? To be victim to this strangling sensation that held reason at bay?

"I'm..." Cam whimpered. He was sagging, rasping, loosing whatever strength remained to him.

Maya reached up with her free hand and took the side of his face. "You're free," she swallowed. He leaned into her touch, nuzzling her palm. The pupil of his uncovered eye shivered, unfocused and dilated from pain, and she watched the amber ring around it lose its light.

The handle of the half-formed knife stopped pulsing, and she let it go. It dissipated in a puff of orange mist, and the gryphon slumped heavily to the ground.

Maya stood for another moment, staring off into nothing, then sank to her knees. She shook uncontrollably, trying to rationalize what had just occurred, but her mind was shut off.

So she wrapped her arms around Camden, buried her face into the last of his warmth, and wept.

The microwave clock read 11:52 P.M. when Maya finally staggered through the front door of her house. Home by Monday night, just as she had promised.

She didn't quite remember how she got there. She knew that Kallot had come by the den as planned, and somehow she had told him what happened, had given him the goblin's belt and the Morning Stone. He had promised to take care of things, had offered her meaningless platitudes. Then she had wandered away from her last ordeal, away from the Fairwoods, and had not looked back.

She made her way into the dark and quiet living room – everyone else was already up in bed – and realized that she was holding Sofia's necklace. She held it up, looked it over, felt it in her hand. Exactly like her own, but entirely separate from it. She understood her sister better now, she thought. She had been given a glimpse of the Heroine's life, and all the wonders it entailed.

But there were more than wonders to such indulgence. What were the thrills of love and excitement when they came burdened with anguish and heartache? Given the option, would anyone truly choose to feel when it was so much easier, so much safer, so much less painful, to forsake sentiment altogether?

Maya looked down at her clothes. They were dirty, torn, and stained with at least three types of blood. She should have been stressed by the necessity of their disposal, by the urgency to get clean, but for once she didn't care. The deluge of emotion had run its course, passed out of her, and left her hollow again. Maybe this time she could make sure it stayed that way.

She opened the grate over the fireplace and set a log within it, then retrieved the matchbook from the endtable by the couch. She withdrew a match, struck it, and tossed it into the pit.

The flames came quickly to life, roasting the air before her. She slipped off her ring and tightened her hand around it, gazing at the flickering, volatile brightness. Then she loosened her grip and looked one more time at the soft golden gleam in her hand.

And she took the ring in her fingers. And held it above the fire. And took a deep breath.

And hesitated.

Acknowledgements

I would like to extend my sincere thanks to Matt Price for patiently enduring my incessant rambling throughout the editing and finalization process of this novella, as well as my other test readers, Sam, Shauna, Dylan, Leslie, Jen, Seth, and Chris.

I must also express my gratitude to you, for spending a slice of your valuable time with me and my silly stories.

About the Author

A former network administrator and software developer for the U.S. Department of Defense, A.L. Walton (otherwise known as Piscis – or simply "the fish") currently resides in Boise, Idaho, where he spends a good chunk of his time making stuff up and putting it on paper. And writing music. But mostly the other thing.

You can follow the author at www.writingfish.net or @TheSpaceFish on Twitter.